6 X 9/08 ✓ 12/08

JACK FISH

ALSO BY J MILLIGAN

The Wisdom of Big Bird
(and the Dark Genius of Oscar the Grouch):
Lessons from a Life in Feathers
(with Caroll Spinney)

JACK FiSH

a novel

J MILLIGAN

SOHO

Copyright © 2004 by J Milligan

Published by
Soho Press, Inc.
853 Broadway
New York, NY 10003

Library of Congress Cataloging-in-Publication Data

Milligan, J.
Jack Fish: a novel/J Milligan.
p.cm.
ISBN 1-56947-382-X (alk. paper)
1. Atlantis—Fiction. 2. Assassins—Fiction. 3. Lost continents—
Fiction. 4. Brooklyn (New York, N.Y.)—Fiction. I. Title.
PS3613.I5628J33 2005
813'.6—dc22   2004048190

10 9 8 7 6 5 4 3 2 1

Jack walked out of the sea.

They had told him to take it slow, to appear to float in after a long swim. "Just sort of drift in to shore on your back," they had said, right before the Big Kiss that oxygenated his blood and the slap on the tush that sent him on his way. Jack tried. He tried to be patient and let the choppy waves push him all the way in, but as soon he sensed that he could stand with his head above water, he charged through the slosh under the pier and didn't stop until he was in the air from his ankles to his hair. That was as far as Jack got before he had to put a hand out to hold on to one of the pilings for balance. He was brought up short by the force of the currents that were pouring down the beach and into the ocean—the overwhelming wash that tried to push him back out to the dark rhythm and brine.

He was first assaulted by the lights. Hundreds of them. Thousands. Flashing ones. Moving ones. Neon, incandescent, fluorescent, dim, bright, on, off. Lights that spelled words, lights that pointed to things and places, lights that illuminated the immediate for only an instant and thereafter sent their energy to the far corners of the universe at the Speed of Light. They had warned him not to stare at them, but he was fascinated by the way they looked—bright, unfiltered, honest. They burned with dazzling zigzags that hung like jellyfish.

He closed his eyes, and he concentrated on the dry wood of the piling—its crisp feel, its sharp outline and solid form. He took the first breath of air through his nose.

He choked.

Jack fell to the sand, clutching his face and throat, coughing, gagging on the air. It burned. His tongue felt like a stone pulled from a fire, his lungs rebelled in sharp, tight contractions. Jack's diaphragm began to seize, and as he hacked, he brought up a sour mouthful of his celebration dinner from the night before. He allowed his legs to give way, and he fell back into the ocean, plunging his face into the water. Jack lay there with his feet splayed out in the line of high-tide seaweed and Styrofoam, the wavelets lapping at his back. He breathed deeply, and slowly stopped sputtering.

A while later he tried another breath, mixing it with water to get it down. He did this a few times, and then flipped over on his back, drawing air in through clenched teeth and exhaling it through pursed lips. It hurt, but he could do it. Jack smiled. After all the training and the chanting, the lectures and the films, he was finally up there—up *here*. The classroom simulations were touching the elephant seal blind, getting a sense of the nose or the tail or the odor in little compartmen-talized experiences. Now he was riding the damn thing.

He had to stop metaphoring. It distracted him from his priorities:

1. Learn to breathe.
2. Find Victor Sargasso.
3. Kill him.

Better take them one at a time, he thought, timing his inhalations and exhalations to the rhythm of the waves. It went OK, got better, even.

"Hey dude! Dude! Are you all right?" A teenaged couple walked hand-in-hand along the beach, looking for a place to get cozy in the sand. What they found instead was Jack, shivering in his regulation deep-blue mankini, sucking air like a Lamaze Yogi.

"Hey! Yo, floating guy!" The boy tried to get Jack's attention. The girl wasn't sure they should mess with a wheezing man bobbing in a tangle of garbage and seaweed.

"He looks like Jesus," she whispered. "Let's just leave him alone."

Jack sensed her discomfort and tried to dispel it. "It's cool! Don't worry about—*hack*—me! I'm just learning to breathe!" He began to choke on the dry, dry air all over again. "I'm—*akk*—OK! Really! I'm cool!—*retch*—Lemme just—" and he plunged his head under the water for relief. When he resurfaced, the young couple was gone.

Jack kept his eyes closed and faced the beach, letting the sounds and smells buffet his face in a sensory storm—he heard the white noise of the waves hitting the sand and voices warning about the undertow and screams set to the arythmic clatter of the old wooden roller coaster and squeaking brakes and honking horns and tinny scraps of carnival music and the cartoon impacts of bumper cars and a Babel of voices casting fishy lies into the water on kite string and twine from the pier above; and he smelled sausages and pink-spun sugar and urine and sunscreen and beer and the acrid sweat of captive Belugas in the aquarium and the smoky boredom from the freakshow and fried clams and popcorn and car exhaust and fear and joy and anger and love—and Jack's knees gave way as the pressure of it all pushed him over and down under the water, again where he could watch the sand move back and forth, and everything was green and blue and gray and brown.

Jack bobbed to the surface. He lay in the water, just breathing. Jack found that he was able to control the ragged flow of air as long as that was the only thing he did with his mind. Speculating on what he would do for the next days or weeks made him go twitchy and his breathing short and shallow, which led right back to the hacking. He reminded himself that he was on track. He was following the standard procedures for an Agent—the Left Prong of the Trident of Atlantis—on his First Ascent:

Make landfall.

He'd done that.

Find the Mermaid Diner.

That was all he had, so that was all he had to worry about. If he stayed with the breathing, the smells and the lights would work themselves out.

There was an empty seat at the end of the counter, and Jack took it, sitting down with a slurpy gasp. His hair and skin were still wet; he was breathing like an asthmatic with a bong stuck in his trachea. He had a plastic coffee-lid stuck to his back, and the only thing he was wearing was his tiny blue mankini. Doris rolled her eyes, sighed, and walked down to Jack's end of the counter. She handed him a menu, and with deft sleight of hand, replaced his list of specials with a handwritten card.

"Welcome to the *Mermaid*," Doris said significantly.

"Good. I'm in the right place," Jack rasped. Then he fell forward, unable even to choke. His throat had shut completely.

"Quick," Doris hissed. She was prepared. She handed him a glass of oxygenated water and a bowl. "Go to the men's room!" Jack hesitated. "Now!" She spun Jack on his stool and pushed him toward the bathroom. He staggered across the floor leaving soggy footprints, which, if looked at carefully, revealed the slight webbing between his toes.

Jack banged through the men's room door and felt like he'd suddenly descended twelve feet into a tropical sea. The sounds from the diner were muffled, as if heard through a couple of fathoms of seawater. The color of the tile perfectly matched Jack's bathing suit. The only source of illumination was the muted light from the street outside, which swept in through the frosted glass at irregular intervals as cars went by. Jack careened off the sink. The glass and bowl flew from his hands and smashed in a puddle of shards. Jack fell to his knees, sucking in through crisp lips.

"Fucking air! Aah!"

He remembered his training:

"OK. Concentrate . . . Focus . . . Control . . . In . . . Out . . . In . . ." He choked, gasped, and then held his breath.

He crouched in the wet pieces of broken dishes. Jack's chest, diaphragm, and buttocks clenched as he tried to hold back the spasms, but he knew as soon as he took another breath, he would begin hacking again, probably even more violently than before. Jack let a little air slip in through his parched mouth, and the pain of it hitting his throat pitched him forward. His guttural cry and retch echoed in the bowl; and his nose dipped into the cool water below. Jack plunged his entire face into the toilet, dragging in relief and exhaling great bubbly wafts. Finally, he pulled himself upright, and sat back on his heels, dripping and sniffing and blinking his eyes. The climate in the room was moist and cool, and the sounds of the cars on the road reverberated soothingly against the tiled walls. Jack became lulled by the humid vibe and his head sank sleepily. *No! I am on a mission!* he reminded himself.

He shook off his reverie, stood up, and faced the mirror over the sink.

Jack looked into his wide-set and bloodshot green eyes, winked, and smiled. His brown hair was matted, his lips were cracked, his skin had a greenish tinge, but for the first time since he had surfaced, Jack felt like he could make it. He turned to the paper towel dispenser. It bore a rusted scar in the shape of a trident, just like the blue tattoo on his shoulder blade. It pointed to a neatly-folded T-shirt and a pair of jeans that some-one had left for him on top of the dispenser. He took down the clothes, put on the pants and the I ♥ NY shirt, and he wiped his face with a stiff, brown paper towel that absorbed almost nothing. Then he took another paper towel from the dispenser and soaked it under the faucet. Respirator in hand, Jack left the submarine isolation of the men's room and shambled back to his stool. As he sat down, his feet found their way into a pair of thoughtfully-placed orange flip-flops. He squeezed the nubbins between his toes. They made his webs itch.

"No shirt, no shoes, no service . . ." quipped Doris, with a meaningful elevation of her left eyebrow. Her words had an immediate effect on Jack, as if his dial had been left between stations, and Doris had just this moment tuned one in, loud and clear.

"Right, uh . . ." Jack fumbled for the proper response. *Ah!* "What's good tonight? Is the fresh fish *fresh*?" He had to emphasize the proper words in the proper way.

"Sure the fresh fish is *fresh*. It's *fresh* fish, ain't it?"

"Hmm. OK. Maybe I'll have a *burger*. And a cup o' *chowder*."

Doris had her thumb on the button that would shoot a poisoned dart from under the counter directly into Jack's abdomen. He had to answer the next question correctly. If he said the wrong thing, she would kill him, that's just how it was. *Too bad if I hafta,* she thought. *He's kinda cute.*

Doris asked, "Manhattan or New England?"

This was it. Jack knew that he might not walk out of the diner if he picked the wrong soup. They had told him which one, but they'd also said that they changed it frequently, to stay one step ahead of the Maltese. Jack knew he had to go with his instinct. And his instinct told him that despite the unconvincing combination of clams and dairy products, New England Clam Chowder was still better than the Manhattan variety.

"*New England . . .*" He closed his eyes and bit down hard. Cutting through the general murmur of the restaurant—

voices complaining about schools and taxes, the mayor, and those pants the kids were wearing these days—he heard a clink, and cautiously opened one eye. There was a steaming cup of creamy soup in front of him. Doris smiled.

"Have a look at our specials, before you go with the *burger*," she suggested firmly and then walked away to refill coffees down the line. The guy at the end with the notebook was shifty and had to be watched.

Jack opened the menu and a note fell into his lap. It was a third- or fourth-generation photocopy, the original version of which had been typed on letterhead bearing a trident-in-a-circle logo. His name had been written in blue ink over Wite-Out, by the same hand that had penned "salisberry steak" and "oriental stur fry" on the actual specials cards clipped to the menu. With great anticipation he read:

A.T. Landis
Swimming Pool Supplies and Filtration Systems

Welcome to the Top Jack Fish and congratulations on completing your ascent. You will be contacted with further information as necessary. Enjoy your meal! Poseidon's blessings,

—mgmt

New York • San Diego • Honolulu • Auckland • Venice • Bombay •
Singapore • Marseilles • Grand Junction • Manila • Vancouver •
Istanbul • Panama City • Halifax • Naples • Miami • Port Au Prince •
Oslo • Hong Kong • Rio de Janeiro

Jack smiled weakly as he balled the paper in his hand and shoved it in his pocket. Of course Sargasso wouldn't be sitting at the counter next to him, sipping tea, waiting to be killed. No, Jack would have to be patient; he had to find his balance before he could strike. There were things for him to do, preparations to prepare, contacts to make, information to gather. But soup? His first act as an Atlantean spy active in the Topworld theater was to eat a bowl of soup?

Yes, he reminded himself, *this is the job. Right now, eating this bowl of soup is the job.*

Jack was suddenly very hungry, and he made quick work of the New England clam chowder. He ordered the fresh fish after all, which turned out to be halibut, and while he waited for the food to arrive, he took surreptitious breaths through his damp paper towel every few minutes to prevent another hacking episode. Doris served him his fish, and said, "Meet me by the Dumpster out back in twenty minutes."

When Jack had eaten his halibut, he got off his stool, inhaled through his moist paper towel, and flip-flopped out the door.

Doris came out the back just as Jack rounded the side of the chrome-paneled diner. She was holding a six-gallon pickle pail brimming over with potato peels, half-eaten egg sandwiches, coffee grounds, and coleslaw. These she scooped off with her left hand and pushed into the Dumpster. She placed the pail on the ground between them and motioned for Jack to hunker down with her.

"OK. Here's the stuff I'm s'posed to give ya," she said as she started pulling things out of the pail and itemizing them for Jack in a bored, singsong voice, placing each thing onto the ground in front of him: "You got your keys to the safe-house, a roll of a thousand US dollars in fives—take it easy when you pull that out—tokens for the subway—a carton of Seaweeds, though I don't know why anyone needs a water-proof cigarette—a Swiss Army knife, the good one with the mini-gaff and the nail file—and here . . ." She extracted a light blue Mets backpack from the pail, brushed off a cucumber peel and a teabag. "Put it all in this." She handed the bag over. "When we're finished, turn right, go up two blocks, turn left, and head straight for another two blocks. On your left you'll see Da Wash."

Jack stared at her blankly.

"It's a car wash, OK? Walk around to the side where the cars come out clean, and get in the gray van being dried by the Mexican kids with the towels. That's Dick Global. He'll take you over by where you'll be stayin'. Here's the address." She flashed a number and a word on a card, then made it disappear into her apron. "Dick will get you close. You walk from there." She pointed to the I ♥ FISHING key-chain in Jack's lap. "The big key unlocks the front door, the little one opens the basement apartment. There'll be a Chinese take-out menu by the phone. Order fried wontons, Moo Shu Chicken—ask for extra pancakes, they never give you enough—white rice, and a Diet 7UP. Give them the address written on the menu, and tell them your name is Hiram. When the food comes, tell the guy you never ordered the 7UP." Doris looked hard at Jack who was studying the various blades of the Swiss Army knife—the fish-scaler and the tiny magnifying glass.

He met her eye. "Sorry. What was that?"

"Make sure you do read the paper in the cookie, OK, honey?" Doris shook her head. *This one seems really dumb*, she thought. *He's never going to make it.* Well, she figured, once he left the diner, there was nothing she could do, and there'd be another one next week anyway. She reached into her apron and pulled out a brown leatherette wallet. "Open it."

Jack did, and found an Ontario driver's license with his picture on it and his name, "Jack Fish," a Stroll-In Video Store membership card, a scratch-off lottery ticket with the silver parts scratched and no prize showing, and a WCS membership card. He held it up and asked, "What's this?"

"Wild Conservation Society or sumthin'. Makes it look like you're a nice guy, like you like animals. Gets you in to the Zoo and the Aquarium for free." Doris dug back into her apron pocket, "Here." She handed him a wad of Landis business cards. "You're in sales, swimming pools or sumthin'."

Jack took a hit through his soggy paper towel. Doris looked at him with her head tilted. "OK?"

"Yeah. OK." Jack wasn't as sure as he had been.

"I've seen guys a lot worse off than you. You'll do fine," Doris lied encouragingly and picked up her empty pickle pail.

Jack shrugged. He loaded up his backpack, and stood up. "Hope so."

They shook hands, and as Jack turned to go, Doris yelled, "Run!"

He ran. Head down, flip-flops flopping, immediately hyperventilating, but moving faster than he thought he could. He heard the bright clatter of a knife bouncing on concrete behind him, and risked a look over his shoulder. Doris was tangled up with the guy who'd been sitting at the end of the counter, blocking his eyegouge with the blade of her hand extending from her nose while she swept at his knees with her leg. Jack felt adrenalin surge through his blood. *The Maltese? Already?* He ran faster.

When he figured he was far enough away, Jack slowed from a full-on flee to a more conservative hurry. He was bewildered, ill, chafing about the thighs, underinformed, a measly pawn in a game he didn't understand—and he felt deliciously free. Jack would have whistled, had his dried-out lips been able to do it, but instead sang a song he had known as a boy at school:

> *Aquaquatic ancients*
> *Terra's flooded basement*
> *We shall rise again!*

Rise again? Jack thought. *That's not going to happen.* The Elders were all about hiding Atlantis at the bottom of the sea, and keeping it hidden. They tended to hide themselves, too—he'd seen them, what, twice? At the exams before spy school and then at graduation. The rest of the time it was "The Elders this, the Elders that" from his professors and TAs. But Jack wasn't going to worry over the politics of his homeland. He was a spy, with a roll of cash and the keys to the safehouse in his pocket—he figured that had to mean chicks. He sang:

> *Flotsam Jetsam*
> *Come on and get some,*
> *The tide will change*
> *And rearrange*
> *For we shall rise again!*

Jack was on his own in Brooklyn, off to meet his driver at the car wash. Atlantis was way behind him somewhere, deep under the sea.

The "NY—See Ya" Car Club had spent the afternoon at Da Wash getting detailed, Simonized and high-pressure undercleaned. Jack crept past their oxymoronic rides—Civics with 17-inch wheels and adenoidal mufflers, Blazers dropped down to three inches ground clearance, pickups with their beds sealed off in paint-matching fiberglass—all getting hydroshammy rubdowns from the boys in the drying department. No gray van, though. He peered into Da Wash, and watched as it disgorged a monochromatic yellow Mustang that read CUM RIDE MY BANANA across the top of its windshield to mad claps and hoots and shouts of "Yo, my nigga!"

Jack went around to the entrance side of the long cinderblock building, but the van wasn't among the car service Town Cars or pimped-out Lexi SUVs lined up for the six dollar wash either. It was parked at a hydrant. This had to be the one—a primer gray Econoline 250 with DICK GLOBAL ENT. BKLYN 11211 stenciled with black spray paint on the doors and DICKVAN plates.

Jack hung back. Maybe he was being followed. But by whom? The ladies with the head-scarves and the over-bundled children? The kids on the corner sucking down fruit punch soda and squinting from under their too-low ban-dannas and big round caps? Jack tried to open the passenger-side door of the van, but it was locked, and he couldn't see much through the deep-tinted window. He went around to the driver's side and put his face up to the glass. A stocky-looking white guy, Dick, he guessed, was slumped in the dri-ver's seat with his bare feet on the dashboard and a half-eaten hot dog resting on his shirt. He was either asleep or dead. Jack hoped the former. He rapped on the window to find out. Dead, it seemed. Jack banged harder, and Dick moved slightly, then woke up in a hurry. He shuddered, flailed his limbs, then put his face to the window, immedi-ately opposite Jack's. Dick motioned for Jack to go around to the passenger side. Then he found his hot dog and promptly forgot about Jack, who had to knock again to get Dick to unlock the door.

"Hey man! I'm Dick! C'mon in the DickVan! You didn't see any Maltese, didja?"

Jack got in and shut the door. "I saw some old ladies back there—"

"No, really. Didja see any of them?"

"Well, there was this one guy at the diner—"

"Dick hears you. Dick's got it under control."

He started the motor, jumped the curb, and slid into first place in line.

"You got any cash?"

"But—?"

"The DickVan's dirty, brah, and we can't have that! It's six bucks, plus a dollar seventy-five for a tree. Mine's stale." Dick yanked down the blue air freshener from his rear view mirror and threw it over his shoulder. He had the DickVan in neutral and the front wheels locked into the carwash tracks before Jack could protest.

Instead, he looked around the DickVan. Every surface—the dashboard, the doors, the ceiling—was completely covered with a collage of taped-up pictures and stuck-on stickers. Posters from *Chitty Chitty Bang Bang* and *Fitzwilly* and *Divorce, American Style* cataloged Dick Van Dyke's career. There was Dick Butkis, from his playing days to distinguished commentator, a cast picture from *Eight is Enough*, the van from the *A-Team*, Dick Gregory, the Mystery Machine, an autographed eight-by-ten of some clown—Dick Monday—Magic Dick from J. Giles, a bumper sticker that read IF THE VAN IS ROCKIN' DON'T COME KNOCKIN', Tricky Dick in his victory pose. A lot of Dicks, a lot of vans, and a few DickVans.

Dick was frantically looking in his mirrors. "It'll be safe to talk once we're inside."

"Talk about what?"

But Dick put a finger to his lips. The van passed through canvas flaps into a soapy monsoon. "Man, you guys are cool," Dick said. "Come up from the depths, take care of any motherfucker thinks they figured you out."

Jack gave Dick a practiced confused look and yelled over the noise of the wash, "I sell pool filtration equipment. My company is based in Toronto. Let me give you my card." He rummaged around in his pockets.

"Wait. Lemme put on some music so they can't hear what we're talking about."

Jack looked up, alarmed. "What are *you* talking about? *We're* not talking about anything! *You're* supposed to drive me somewhere, right?"

Dick fished around under his seat, came up with some tapes, rejected Van Morrison, popped Dick Dale into the deck, and surf guitar rippled through the van.

"No, come on, is it like Plato says, or Cayce?" Dick yelled over the racket of water thudding on the metal roof.

"Wha?"

"And where is it? The Azores? The Bahamas? Or that Iceland theory? Personally, I think that one's bullshit. Hey, are the Maltese really the guys who got off Atlantis before it sank? And did you guys really build all the pyramids, the Egyptian ones *and* the ones in Mexico?"

Jack realized that Dick was TCGWALI—The Curious Guy With A Little Info. Jack had been prepped for this. He said, "Look, when someone starts to figure it out, maybe we let 'em get a few things right, so they start out looking good, like they're on to it. Then the Information Ministry feeds them some garbage, so they get written off as cranks. Works every time."

"But Plato?"

"He's all metaphor, right? Parable, whatever. 'Beyond the gates of Hercules, 900 Stadia.' Sure, fine. It's true enough.

Now go ahead and use the *Critias* to find anything. Nobody's done it yet."

"Uh-huh. So what about that secret metal you guys got? And what about the Stars? Those energy-source crystal thingies?"

"You know I can't tell you about any of that."

"Nice. Keep it on the q.t.d.l., know what I'm sayin'?"

"Uh-huh." Jack didn't at all.

Floppy rubber tentacles slapped the DickVan with whomping sudsy belts that rang loudly inside its metal box. More water came down to rinse the soap off, and high pressure hoses blasted at the wheels and tires. The DickVan inched forward through the wash, at a pace that felt slower to Jack than his ascent to the top. They were pulled under huge blowdryers that chased beads of water up the windshield, and after passing through another curtain of rubber strips, the DickVan was in the open air, being swaddled by the Mexican boys with their towels. Dick tipped them with Jack's change, purchased his new little tree, hung it from the mirror, and pulled onto the sidewalk, where he stopped.

"New-Car smell! That's the flavor of the blue ones. Makes the DickVan smell like a new car! Sweet, right?"

"Uh, Dick. Could we get out of here? I think we should go."

"Right on, dude. We're gone! Just lemme get my shoes on."

Dick grabbed the pair of black-and-white-checked Vans that had been sitting on the dash, pulled them onto his bare and bunioned feet, and dropped the DickVan into gear. He hit the streets, heading for Coney Island Avenue.

A few carlengths behind, a matte-black Buick GNX

accelerated out from between a blue Infiniti Q with gold accents and a Geo Tracker with tires that stuck out a foot beyond the frame on both sides. The Buick growled, barely drawing on its two turbo units, a sinister brick of Detroit steel and dumb power. The two men inside wore identical black suits, white shirts, and gold ties. The passenger spoke in Latin into a cell phone; the driver drove. A small red flag emblazoned with a diagonal white stripe and a gold cross emblem fluttered from the antenna.

In the passenger seat of the DickVan, Jack wobbled, swayed from the waist, and gasped. All the saliva in his mouth wicked through his cheeks, and was gone. His tongue fused to his palate and stuck there. "Ghhhh," he said.

Dick heard him.

"I hear ya. In the back. Got a case of Gatorade. Git yourself one."

Jack nodded, clambered over the hot transmission hump, and fell onto Dick's semi-inflated fuckmat with a flat thump. The air around him fooled his muscle memory and inner ears. The absence of pressure, the cubic emptiness, caused him to move too abruptly, overcompensating for his actions. He was dizzy and nauseous. His head flopped from shoulder to shoulder with every change in the DickVan's deltavee. Images of the borough flashed in his eyes:

RESTAURANT PUNJABI RIMS LUBE SHOCKS CAR ON SIDEWALK PREGNANT WOMAN SCREAMING RENT ME!

FAT MAN SELLING ICE CREAM NO MONEY DOWN!
INSPECTION STATION MIXED NUTS TORAH ACADEMY
99 CENTS

Jack knew what was wrong with his equilibrium. He had
the classic symptoms. They had warned him to expect it.

"Whaleshit," he swore. "I'm landsick."

"Landsick? Oh crap." Dick had forgotten that this was
likely to happen. He'd seen it before. "Dick's got something
here for ya. Forgot. Sorry."

He leaned toward his glove compartment and poked at
the cantankerous latch. The DickVan swerved mercilessly
into oncoming traffic as Dick's attention dropped below the
dashboard. The sudden shift threw Jack back to the fuckmat. After a sharp chop with the side of Dick's hand, the
glove box flopped open and with thumb and forefinger
extended, Dick extracted a hypodermic loaded with something bright red-orange.

"Dick's got what you need right here, man."

Jack peered dubiously over the seat.

"What's that? Oh. . ." Jack considered the chemical sta-
bility the shot would deliver, but chose to act stoic and pro-
fessional. "No. I'm going to ride this out. I don't want to get
all confused just when I'm getting started."

Dick shrugged and carefully stuck the syringe behind his
ear. "Whatev. It's here when you want it." He steered the
DickVan back into the appropriate lane.

Unable to sit up reliably, Jack rolled around the back of the
van until his head bonked into the side of a red plastic Igloo
cooler. He slid the top open and pulled a dripping bottle from

the slush inside. Still on his back, Jack held the plastic nipple between his teeth, pulled, and squeezed a jet of sweet, salty, and sour wet electrolytes at his epiglottis. Startled, he squinted at the label.

"Fierce Melon? What *is* this?"

"All the bold flavor you can handle, brah."

Thwack! A gold-tipped harpoon punctured the steel skin of the back door of the DickVan and with a shudder and a twang embedded itself in the rear of the passenger seat Jack had recently occupied. Jack tumbled to the left as Dick belatedly swerved.

"What was that?" Jack yelled, facedown on the fuckmat.

Dick confirmed his guess with a glance in the mirror.

"Harpoon. Maltese. After us. Hang on."

He gunned the DickVan, and briefly kept it up as if he thought he could outrun his pursuers. The GNX gained rapidly, whining turbos forcing cylinders to gulp more air.

"Hang on back there!" Dick shouted.

"To what?"

Dick began evasive maneuvers, which were indistinguishable from his normal driving habits—sudden lane changes, abrupt acceleration, erratic swerving.

He grumbled, "Fucking Illuminati eye-in-the-pyramid motherfuckers. Ain't gonna outrun their equipment in no Econoleen. Gotta try the Battlestar Galactica moves."

The Maltese changed lanes and came up alongside the DickVan. Dick waited for them to match speeds. He kept an eye on the Goldtie in the passenger seat of the GNX, who was aiming a harpoon at the DickVan's front left tire. Dick revved, as if trying to eke every drop of speed from his engine, then stomped on the brakes stopping the DickVan cold. A harpoon clattered across the hood and whizzed through the hole in an eight-foot-high promotional bagel. The GNX roared away. Jack was thrown against the back of the front seats, then hurled off and tumbled around the rear of the van like a baby turtle in the churn as Dick pulled a hard Brooklyn U, cutting across the Avenue and headed back toward Coney Island and the sea.

"Come on back up here and have a seat. Pull the spear out first, though, brah."

Jack yanked the heavy shaft and cruel, barbed tip through the back of the seat in a burst of crusty foam and placed it carefully against the side of the van. Then he scrambled over the hump and dropped in against the cracked vinyl and unwound springs of the upholstery. He put on his seatbelt to hold him in place while his head lolled around. Peering down with one eye open, Jack noticed he was still clutching the Gatorade. He took another long pull through the Sport Top, swallowed, and let out a satisfied, "Aaah!" before remarking, "Fierce Melon! In the DickVan!"

Dick agreed, "Fierce Melon. In the DickVan," then he checked his mirror. The GNX was a dark smudge behind them.

He said, "Dick don't know the back of his hand, but Dick sure as fuck knows Brooklyn better than those crypto-motherfuckers." He made an illegal right on red into the gray closeness of the sidestreets.

Jack saw:

BOYS WITH SKULLCAPS LONG COATS FRINGE UNDER
DIRTY SHIRTS LOTTO LOTTO LIQUOR WINES VANTAGE

MONARCH LLENO DE GUSTA AUTO GLASS HALAL
MEAT FLAT DEAD BIRD SCHOOL BUS BEST DEAL CAM-
ERA 19.99 AVENUE J AVENUE I BAIL BONDS SCUBA
CAFÉ BUSTELO

Dick was talking, " . . . people say not to take the BQE,
but the streets— fuck that, with all the construction and that
water main break by the Navy Yard. So it slows down by the
Brooklyn Bridge, so what? Dick says, take the outside lane
and you get by sooner or later. But today, change of plans,
Dick is going deep to lose those gold-wearing freaks . . .
Jack? Jack?"

Time had almost completely stopped for Jack.

He was watching a dog—

    squat and strain   squat and strain   squat and
    strain   squat and strain   squat and strain
      squat and strain   squat and strain

"Nothing is coming out," he marveled.

"OK. That's it. You need to take your medicine." Dick
plucked the hypo from behind his ear and spiked it into Jack's
thigh. Jack's body hinged closed at the waist, rigid in pain,
until Dick slammed the plunger down with the heel of his
hand and warm well-being spread outward from Jack's leg
down to his foot, around his groin to his other leg and up his
trunk to his arms, neck, face, and scalp, enveloping him in an
orange cloud of sharp confidence and positive energy. His
right hand grabbed his buzzing genitals as his left hand found
the Gatorade in the cupholder and brought it to his lips.

"Yah! Fierce Melon!" He pulled a swig. "Aaah! Fierce Melon in the DickVan! Right?"

Dick smiled at Jack, pulled the empty needle out of his leg and tossed it over his shoulder. "You got that right. Fierce Melon in the DickVan!"

Jack laughed. "I mean, what the hell is a fierce melon? Not like a gentle melon, a passive melon, some kind of submissive guppy melon. Fierce Melon! Yeah! This melon is aggro man, a warrior melon, a super-spy melon, a melon not to be fucked with. Because it's fierce! Fierce Melon!"

"Fierce Melon!" echoed Dick.

The first wave of the shot subsided. The second carried Jack up a gentler, longer slope to a place with better perspective. He let go of his package as he remembered the Maltese trying to kill him. The Maltese—the ancient enemies of his people, bent on exposing Atlantis, and in fact the only sovereign entity that knew his people existed—he had expected to have to deal with them at some point, but not as soon as he arrived. They must have better intelligence than the Elders had guessed.

"Did we lose them?"

"I think so. Haven't seen them since Avenue P, but who knows with those motherfuckers? Maybe they want us to think they're gone, maybe they are, maybe they're not. I'm taking the scenic route to the drop. If they turn up again, we head for Jersey."

"What's in Jersey?"

"My mother."

Dick didn't have to resort to New Jersey. He picked a

route through bad neighborhoods and worse ones, took parkways, expressways, and local streets, doubled back on himself, drove the full loop around Prospect Park, negotiated the complicated merges under the BQE, connected with Kent Avenue, and followed it north. Jack could smell the dark, tough East River close by.

They passed the entire block of Domsey's used clothing warehouses, went under the Williamsburg bridge, past a bohemian bar and a Mafia restaurant, finally stopping at a tiny park squeezed between an oil refinery and the Domino sugar plant. They got out of the van and sat on a bench, watching the dockworkers unload a freighter from the Dominican Republic. The sun had set, and they worked under floodlights. Jack squinted at the illuminated stir in the choking river.

He was beyond tired. His voice was strained from the yelling and the coughing, which threatened to erupt again at any moment. The power plant across the river made a neutral focal point. Jack watched it pump smog into the atmosphere from its four towering smokestacks.

Dick said, "This is as far as Dick takes you. Now, Dick gets back in the DickVan and drives away. You're almost there. Then you can relax, breathe some water, do whatever it is you dudes do."

Jack nodded. He reached out to steady himself and put a hand on Dick's shoulder. He had come all the way back down from the shot, and was now headed lower. The landsickness was still there, only partially obscured behind his increasing exhaustion and anxiety.

"You're gonna be fine, man. Shit, coming from where you come from, you're gonna be fine."

"What in Hades was in that shot?" Jack asked quietly.

Dick laughed. "Placebo. Sugar water. Nothing but—"

"Gatorade." Jack finished for him, shaking his head in disbelief. "You shot me up with Fierce Melon."

"In the DickVan!" Afraid that Jack would hit him, Dick tried to inspire another rousing chant. "Fierce Melon in the DickVan?"

"Fierce Melon in the DickVan," Jack sighed, and he started laughing.

Dick joined in, and the two of them laughed and laughed, until Jack began a coughing jag so violent that he had Dick pick him up by his ankles and dunk him in the river to make it stop. The dockworkers took a break from the canejuice hoses to throw pennies at his head.

J ack stood squinting under the streetlights at the corner of Metropolitan and Wythe. The things inside his head felt much too large for the skull that held them. An urban tumbleweed of a plastic grocery bag puffed down the street on light gusts of dry wind and wrapped itself around Jack's ankle. Jack pulled it off, and looked at it. I ♥ NY, just like his shirt. What did that mean? Jack had noticed an I ♥ALLAH sticker on a cab. It had barely registered, but now he wanted one very badly. For what? He could get a car to put it on, one of those large boxy '80s Caprices he'd seen, favored by car service guys and Hasidic Jews. Jack thought he could live here somewhere in the outer boroughs and drive around in his undershirt, double-park in front of delis, and smoke Newports . . . maybe that could be his mission. Jack began to hack again. People walked around him without paying any attention. Well,

that was good. At least he blended in—it was a whole neighborhood of people who looked like they had just washed up
from the bottom of the sea.

Jack found the building—asbestos-shingled in green and
sagging to the left, built cheap on speculation in the years
just before completion of the Williamsburg bridge. He began
to cough in rapid-fire bursts, broken by big, rattling gasps.
The key turned easily in the Mul-T-lock, and he stepped
around the door, slamming it shut behind him, then using it
to prop himself up. "Basement apartment. OK, must be
down," Jack muttered, steeling himself.

The stairs were covered in layers of torn vinyl flooring,
each in a garish discount color that clashed with the strata
below it— Granite Sunrise over Desert Rose over Hula Hoop
over Cornflower over Puce. They were all ugly. A single low-
watt bulb hung begrudgingly over the landing, casting a faint
cone of light. The smell of mildew was thick in the shadows.

Jack took the steps, relying heavily on the wiggly banister
caked with latex enamel that hid the lead-based paint
beneath. He descended into must and the reek of cat piss.
Leaning heavily against the unpainted steel door, he keyed
the lock and fell into the safehouse, counterintuitively num-
bered apartment 12L.

It was a railroad layout—three low rooms in a row, with
tiny windows near the ceiling on either end, a scuffed blue
linoleum floor, cheerful disposable Swedish furniture with
the tags still on, and a 27-inch Sony tube with cable. The
only thing Jack cared about, though, was the bottle of Evian,
the steel bowl, and the pink towel, strategically laid out on
the floor five feet from the door. He poured the water into

the bowl and immersed his face in French Alpine spring water until the burning stopped. French water, that came in plastic bottles from across the ocean, over fathoms and fathoms of more water, over the heads of the unseen citizens of the deep. Jack sucked bubbles through it and pictured a ship with a hold full of Evian sailing over the waves in a driving rain.

Jack walked around his new place. The kitchen was clean enough, though it seemed from lack of use, rather than the regular attention of disinfectant sprays and paper towels. A Björk table and three Björn chairs sat in a patient group in the middle of the space, next to fifteen-year-old appliances. Toward the front of the building there was another room. It had three substantial things in it: the big, black television, which was on with the sound muted; a Tabla glass-topped coffee table with clever beech veneer shelves to hold videotapes and shelter magazines; and a beige Tüshî sofa that converted into a double guest bed. Jack dropped his backpack on the table and walked back through the kitchen to the bedroom.

There was a Smeg futon bed, a Stüff set of drawers, and a couple of doors that, when opened, led to a tiny bathroom and a walk-in closet. Done with the tour, Jack returned to the front room. He sat down on the Tüshî, and put his feet up on the Tabla. John Johnson's giant head silently yammered at him from the TV, reporting on the scene in Far Rockaway, where another whale had beached itself for reasons nobody understood. Jack reached for the remote on the table. It was sitting on a menu, and that's when Jack remembered what the waitress had said behind the diner.

Jack found the phone and the Chinese take-out menu under it and made the call.

"HoWokholdplease," somebody answered.

Jack had to remember the correct order. *Sesame Chicken and Moo Goo Gai Pan? Oyster Pancake and Shanghai Soup Dumplings? Rib Tips and Happy Family? Dragon and Phoenix? Drunken Crab?* He had to dig deep, regress, rewind the memory tape the way they had taught him. *Live it again, there was Doris, the Dumpster . . .*

"Ho Wok, whatsyouaddress? Address?"

Jack panicked. Then he looked at the menu in his lap. Somebody had helpfully written it there for him.

"Whatsyouorder?"

"OK. It's, uh . . . ." Jack rolled his eyes back in his head and hoped it would come out right: "Fried . . . wontons. Moo Shu . . . Chicken. Oh! With extra pancakes, please."

"Extra pancake cost twenty-five cent. Each one.

"OK. And may I have a Diet 7UP?"

"Diet 7UP? Nobody wantthat! OK. I giveittoyou, no problem. What'syouname?"

"It's uh . . . Hi . . . Hi . . . Hiram. Yeah. Hiram."

"Hiram? You sound different! OK. Yougotit! DuckSoyMustad?"

"What?"

"You want sauce? DuckSoyMustad?"

What was the answer? Doris hadn't mentioned the sauce. Jack's eyes rolled forward and opened wide. *The sauce?* This could be like the soup. Answer wrong, and they slip something besides MSG into your Moo Shu. Again, Jack had to go with his gut, and his gut said, "Sure."

"Fifteen minute." The Ho Wok hung up. Jack clicked off the TV's mute, and found a channel that showed Jacques Cousteau documentaries. He dozed on the Tüshî until the door buzzer buzzed.

"Ten forty-three," said the delivery fellow. He gave Jack the eyeball and shook the receipt, which was stapled to the bag.

Jack gave him three fives off his roll, then remembered to check his order. He opened the bag. "What's this? I never ordered this!" He held up the diet 7UP with two fingers, a look of disgust on his face.

"Why you guys always do this? Why you don't just ask for cookie?" The delivery fellow handed Jack a fortune cookie from his pocket, made no attempt to make change, and left.

Jack pulled the containers out of the bag. The Ho Wok had forgotten the sauces. A mistake, a sign, or what? Jack looked at the sweating can in his hand. *Why* do *we ask for Diet 7UP?* He put down the can, and opened the stapled Styrofoam clamshells. Jack was very hungry, despite having eaten at the diner, and was comforted by the familiar sight of bean sprouts and shredded chicken—take-out Chinese food looked about the same above the sea as it did below. He feasted on the wontons and Moo Shu while Jacques Cousteau looked for giant squid in the Sea of Cortez. "Ze squid zey stay down very deep, and no man knows why," Jacques intoned meaningfully.

Jack groaned, flinging the stale end of a pancake at the screen. Then he fell asleep.

It wasn't until after he'd woken, submerged his head in

the sink, changed into a clean I ♥ NY shirt he found in the drawer next to the Aquaman underoos, and eaten some cold Moo Shu that Jack remembered the cookie. He squeezed it, smashing the cookie and bursting the plastic package with a satisfying pop. He carefully pulled out each lemony splinter and nibbled away. Then he extracted the small ribbon of paper from the torn plastic. Inaction is action, he read.

What am I supposed to do with that? Then he turned the paper over, and read: Ave. B + 13th St. → red door x Frank's Fish → Johnny Belmont. It wasn't Victor Sargasso's address, but it was something.

"Well, I guess that's pretty clear. It's on, baby!"

His voice rang flat against the walls of the apartment, a half-tone off of the sincere, natural coolness he had hoped would lie at the core of his delivery. He felt a little foolish, but whatever embarrassment he suffered was outweighed by an out-of-body moment of perspective: He was doing it, for real, at last. It all led to this, to today. Jack smiled a shy and wise sort of smile. He'd done it. How? This nursery, those friends, that test, lower school, upper school, tapped by someone for something, choices about then that created now? Is that how it always worked? Swim in one direction long enough, and you're not going someplace else? Or would he have wound up here no matter which way he went? Here, cooling out in the safehouse, about to interrogate a guy who might know how to find the rogue agent.

Barnacles. Jack knew he was at a cusp, at the interface between potential and actuality, and he felt absolutely clearheaded, focused, calm. He had ascended from the murky depths, made landfall, found the diner, made his way through Brooklyn, and dealt with the delivery fellow. In a few hours, he would meet—he glanced at the piece of paper—Johnny Belmont, and his mission would manifest itself, crystallize from the gel of possibility, it would *begin,* and he would finally, really become an Agent, the Left Prong of the Trident on the Topworld. Until then he was doing exactly what he was supposed to be doing—watching TV. *This is the job,* he reminded himself. *Watching TV is the job.*

Jack fumbled around in the backpack. He broke out the carton of Seaweeds. He opened a pack, sparked one up, and gagged a bit before getting the rhythm of it—draw, inhale, pause, release, muse. He'd never smoked in Atlantis, but it felt like what a spy would be doing in the safehouse while killing time before meeting his contact. It occurred to him that he had been breathing without coughing for a while. Now he smiled. He lit another Seaweed off the first, and sat back on the Tüshî. There was a show on TV about the Blue Hole off Belize, and Jack laughed, watching the divers do it backwards, going from top to bottom.

Jack had seen a jacket hanging in the closet, a blue canvas Carhartt with his name embroidered above the left breast pocket and A.T. LANDIS POOL SUPPLIES stitched across the back. He put it on. Then he gathered up the smokes, put them back in the Mets backpack, and shouldered it. He opened the door, stepped out into the dim hallway, trying not to gag on the musty air. It was time to meet Johnny Belmont.

J ack easily dodged the prone homeless guy in a NEW YORK FUCKIN' CITY hat who swung at his legs with a broom as he left the subway. The narrow streets of the Lower East Side were viscous in struggle and trade and rotting garbage, the shabby tenements loomed close on either side. There was activity everywhere—men with hollow eyes loitering in doorways, guys looking for drugs, guys looking for buyers, women leaning out of windows calling to people in the street below, guys washing cars and fixing cars and sitting on cars and talking to other guys in cars and driving cars away, entire families sitting on stoops, eating and talking and watching TV, kids chasing dogs, dogs chasing kids, cats and rats and pigeons adapted wild to the environment, people going in and out of grocery stores, and bars, and lounges, and stores that didn't seem to sell anything in particular but had a lot of business.

The neighborhood was like a reef, with apartment buildings serving as the crusty infrastructure and creatures exploiting every available niche, people everywhere filling it with life, making it live. Jack understood it. He could see how interconnected it was, how there was a delicate balance that made it work. If the temperature went up just one degree there would be chaos and widespread death. Jack moved through the teeming streets, touching nothing.

He found the place. The battered red-steel-bomb-shelter door fit the description provided by the fortune cookie. It looked uninviting and unsafe, the kind of place most people would hurry past if they noticed it at all.

Jack stood for a moment outside the bar. He felt the imminent disappointment that comes before opening any door and walking through it. Jack knew that once he did, he would cross the threshold from possibility to a single course of action that would be his story and his fate: becoming an Agent of the Elders of Atlantis. He opened the door and went in.

Inside, no one gave Jack the eyeball, nobody cared who came in, out, whatever, *it's all the same, and none of my business anyway*. The bar was its own crowd filter, its essence more effective than a red velvet rope. Those who felt at home among the roaches, mismatched broken furniture, cinderblock walls, Patty Smith/Patsy Kline/Pogues soundtrack, and the vague glistening moistness that filmed tables, toilets, and every face and glass were welcome to stay as long as they fought somewhere else and paid up before they left. Overwound fast-track brokers, fired newspapermen, squatters from around

the corner, pallid New Media hucksters, the pierced and the
wounded and the angry and the slowly doomed shot pool,
watched the game, borrowed tattered novels from the bar-
keeps, pissed on the walls of the bathrooms, nodded and
grunted greetings and sympathy to one another night after
night after night—

"Pint of dark?"

"Howyadoing, Mac?"

"Fuckin' cops won't leave me alone."

"Got five bucks?"

"Yah, for your Mother."

Jack decided to take a minute to have a drink and get his
spy on before he started working on this Belmont guy. He
spotted a seat at the far end of the bar, but to get there he
would have to negotiate the narrow path of legs, backs,
elbows, and dogs that ran between the bar and the row of
stools against the wall. Jack began the journey, picking his
way along, tapping shoulders gently here and there and ran-
domly mumbling "Excuse me's" and "Pardons." After
some progress, Jack's way was utterly blocked by a man in
a rumpled suit with his hands on his knees, vomiting onto
his shoes.

The man unbent and said helpfully to Jack, "Careful!
Somebody puked on the floor!"

Jack skirted the puddle and also Tonka the pitbull, who
had already begun lapping it up, and made it finally to the
empty seat in the corner. He sat and fell forward with his
face on the bar, gasping and croaking.

Mac the bartender stood before him, unfazed. "Whajalike?"

Jack pointed to the glass belonging to the huge man next to him. It contained twenty brown and frothy ounces.

"Pint of dark?" Mac confirmed, and with Jack's nod, pulled him one.

Jack had had beer before—the Elders had an arrangement with a Greek shipping company and there was a fairly reliable delivery of kegs of pisslite lager that drifted down like depth charges and floated back up empty—but never brew like this. An investigative slurp spoke to Jack's senses of things he had never experienced—unsweetened cocoa, loaves of fresh pumpernickel cooling on racks, a whiff of red meat slowly charring on a grill over a peat fire not far from the sea, the sea, the sea—

Jack swallowed and took a deeper drink, rolling the liquid from cheek to cheek across his tongue, inhaling with his nose in the glass, its tip just touching the surface of the beer. The brew coated his mouth and throat with soothing coolness and gently numbing alcohol. After a few gulps, he was able to breathe without labor or pain.

OK, where is this Johnny Belmont? Jack tried to scope out the crowd, but he was cornered between the antique AC unit that was buffeting the left side of his head with cold, damp air, and an enormous, bitter man who was muttering into his beer. Without turning around, it was nearly impossible for Jack to see anything but the dull mirror and grimy liquor bottles behind the bar. He tried to listen to what was going on around him—the chock of the balls on the pool table, the lamentations of Black 47, the occasional crash of a dropped glass, the debate over the relative quality and economic advantages of domestic versus imported marijuana—

but mostly, Jack's aural sphere was dominated by his giant neighbor, who, as he did every night, was describing his living situation in an unstoppable tirade to no one in particular.

Jack's beer vanished rapidly. Mac's bartender radar sensed this, and Jack nodded to the suggestion of a refill. He figured it was the responsible thing to do. If his throat dried out and the coughing began again, he might have to jump back into the East River and miss meeting his contact altogether.

"Two thousand square feet! That's right! Enough room for a five-generation Dominican family! Uncles and aunts and grandmas and motherfuckin' great-grandmas! All to my goddamned self! Since 1978! And how much do I pay? How *much* do I pay? Four-thousand dollars a month? No!" The big man broke off into cackling laughter, swigged his beer, choked on the foam, and picked up the diatribe where he had left off. "Two-thousand dollars a month? Ha!"

He became aware of Jack to his left, and slowly turned to look at him. He leaned in, peering at Jack through slits of eyes and kept leaning until his fleshy face was mere inches from Jack's. Recognizing Jack to be someone who had not yet experienced his rant, the big guy focused the blast of his harangue on him.

"Remember, on West Broadway, studios go for far more than that. Stupid fucking studios, three hundred square feet with one of those miniature crappy dollhouse stoves that have all four burners next to each other, so if you had, say, a large nonstick pan on there, you know, because you were making some eggs, it would cover all of the burners and you couldn't boil water to make a fucking goddamned cup of tea." He startled himself with this image. "Not a fucking goddamned cup of tea! Howdyalike that for three grand a month?! And I don't pay even one-thousand dollars a month! No way!"

There was a pause while both men drank, then Jack's neighbor resumed: "Let me tell you something. I don't pay one thousand dollars a month, or one hundred dollars a month, or even one dollar a month! I don't pay anything, and I haven't for years, and do you know why? Do you?"

". . ."

"Ventilation! That's why! My landlord doesn't have a C of O for the space! No Certificate of Occupancy! My apartment doesn't have proper ventilation in the bathroom, and that means it can't get a proper C of O, and that means that my crooked cunt of a landlord can't legally charge me rent because *it is not legally an apartment!* And he can't throw me out because I've lived there for more than three months! Three months! Ha! Try twenty years! No rent for twenty fucking years in a two-thousand square foot dream apartment in Soho because there's no fucking fan in the bathroom! So I sit there in a cloud of my own farts—for free! I win!"

The image of a cloud of this man's farts terrified Jack more than his impending mission, and he began to unseat himself from his stool and resume looking for his contact. The giant man wasn't finished with him, though.

"Where are you from?" he wanted to know.

"Canada." That seemed to stop the coversation.

"Oh," said the big man, smiling uncertainly.

Jack smiled and escaped to the back room, the special domain of Balthazar's Spinning Yo-Yo Mystics.

Balthazar—curly-haired, goat-goateed, wizened, barroom

yo-yo sage—Balthazar looked right at Jack and, loud enough to be heard over the Pixies, said, "Jack-be-nimble, Jackie Chan, You don't know Jack, Jackie Childs, that's a fact Jack, Jack Shit, Jack London, Jackie Gleason, Jack Squat, Blackjack, Jack of Spades, Jack!"

Jack was startled, and began looking deep into the corners of the bar, as nonchalant as an awkward guy clearly looking for someone else could be.

"Little Jack Horner sitting in a corner, Jack of all trades, Jack Straw, Jackknife, Jack off, Jack Palance, one-eyed Jack, Jack Kennedy, New Jack City, Jack! I am Balthazar, and I invite you to *come*!" The last syllable was in the imperative, and it drew Jack across the room.

There were six young disciples at Balthazar's table—four men and two women, all clad in long black jackets with white shirts and black pants. All wore tight black skullcaps. Before each was a yo-yo—two were green, two blue, one was orange, and one was black. All had been paying rapt attention to their rebbe, but now were looking at Jack.

"Sit, young Jack."

Jack sat between a man with a green yo-yo and a woman with a black one. He turned to Balthazar.

"How did you know?" he asked.

"Your name? Because it is written on your blue-collar worker-type jacket. This does not matter. What does matter is that I also know that you are from the lost continent that is not lost, incontinent, Atlantis, which is as real a place as Bayonne or Bogota or Lodi or Linden, and even more afraid of what lies above and beyond."

Jack's training fought his hazy limpness, and while his

mind was catching up to Balthazar's compromising pro-
nouncement, his body assumed the first pose in the eons-old
aquatic martial art taught to all Atlanteans before their
twelfth year.

Balthazar laughed. "Relax, my son. For I have no more
desire to expose you and your people than you do to bring
them the news that an old teacher, a Yo-Yo Rebbe, saw from
the moment you entered this place your fishy agenda, your
marine mandate, your recent introduction to the air. Jack,
the man you seek to meet is standing by the jukebox. I think
he is doing his best to meet someone himself. He is failing, of
course. But you have done well tonight, you have begun to
find your way in the world, for here is the world as much as
anywhere else, or at least this is a world and not everywhere
else is either. Here. . ." Balthazar produced a green Duncan
Imperial from his voluminous robe. The yo-yo was a translucent plastic lozenge with DUNCAN IMPERIAL ORIGINAL—
WORLD'S #1 printed across a fleur-de-lis on one side and three
Hebrew characters—בּ ץ ר—on the other. It was cool to the
touch and slightly sticky and fit perfectly into the hollow of
Jack's palm. He took Jack's hands and held them for a
second in his own. Balthazar's knuckles were knobby, but
his skin was surprisingly soft.

"*Kneel*," Balthazar commanded in his commanding voice.
Jack did so, at the rebbe's feet. Balthazar took measure of
Jack's right index finger and, with barely a motion, tied a
knot in the end of the string, slipped it over the string again
to create a slipknot, and placed the loop around Jack's finger.

"The yo-yo has much to teach those willing to learn.
When the finger in the loop is steady, the nature of the yo-yo

is to return to where it begins, no matter how tricky the route. It is when the finger in the loop hesitates that the yo-yo swings and spins and winds up dangling at the end of its string with no momentum to go anywhere at all. I give you the green yo-yo of the novice. Perhaps one day you will be ready for the blue or beyond. You must learn to walk the dog before you may sit with us again. Now go and do what you will, or at the very least, do what you must."

Jack was dismissed. He rose and pocketed his yo-yo, the string still tight around his finger.

Johnny Belmont had chosen his spot next to the juke-box strategically. In this bar, the women were the DJs—the men would pony up the singles, but the women would feed them into the machine and choose the tunes. This meant that by planting his splayed feet, thick frame, and bad suit in one place, Johnny Belmont had an easier time of getting dissed by all of them than if he had to actually walk around and find each one individually. His plan was working perfectly. With the frequency of planes landing at LaGuardia, women approached the jukebox, surveyed the tunes, fed in a few bills, punched the buttons, and told Johnny Belmont to go fuck himself. Johnny Belmont was as wired as an air-traffic controller, and didn't take it personally. Instead, he took nose hits off a small vial he kept in his jacket pocket and propositioned each DJ with offers of weird sex and fondue.

So that's Johnny Belmont, thought Jack. The decrypted receipt for the Chinese food had told him that Belmont had been recruited by Victor Sargasso before he disappeared, that Belmont had been a cop, but had done something idiotic enough to get removed from the force, that Belmont was a man of appetites and easily tempted, and that Belmont owed Landis over twenty thousand dollars, which would be Jack's leverage. He approached the jukebox, feigning interest at the song selection, and nodded at Johnny Belmont who said, "Howyadoing?"

"OK," Jack answered cautiously.

"Not me. Getting pretty fucking thirsty standing here all night," said Johnny Belmont, sniffling as he swiped his index finger under his right nostril.

"Sure. Thirsty work, standing. How 'bout a drink?"

"Good idea!"

Back at the bar, Johnny Belmont waved the barkeep over. "So, Mac," he began, "know what happened to me last night?"

"Last night? You came here, you got drunk, you went home, same as always."

"Not last night! So listen, so I'm sitting right here, minding my own, when this chick, well she wasn't exactly a chick, more like mid-thirties, but really hot, you know, you could tell she worked out, you know, a finestress, yeah? She comes up to me, I'm minding my own, like I said, and she comes up to me and she's like 'hello' and so I'm like 'hello' back, you know? Yeah, and she's like, 'Look man, no bullshit, come home with me, I need it and you look like you can give it to me.' And I'm like 'Holy shit!' I mean, just like that, you know, no what's-a-guy-like-you-doing-in-a-shithole-like-this bullshit—No offense, Mac."

The bartender shrugged.

"No nothing, just 'Come with me, let's fuck,' so I'm like 'Yeah!' I mean, look, why not, you know? She's hot, and why the hell not, you know?" Johnny Belmont rubbed his nose.

Mac looked at Jack. His eyes smiled, maybe in amusement, maybe in mockery, or maybe a little of both. He said to Belmont, "Sure, why not?"

"Sure, fuck it," Belmont said. "I'm going with her, so I do, I mean, yeah, we walk out of the bar, and she grabs a cab, and like when do you see a cab at three A.M.? But whatever, there it is, so we get in, and I don't hear what she says to the driver, we just go, you know? So we start driving, and she doesn't even say anything, she just starts kissing me and putting her hand in my pants and putting my hand up her shirt, and she's not wearing a bra or nothing, and we're like going at it in the fucking cab! But the cabbie says nothing, 'cause like, he's probably seen everything go on in there, orgies and shit, so whatever, so we get to wherever she says and we get out and she pays, and I don't even know where we are, like maybe the Upper East, or somewheres, and she takes my hand, and leads me upstairs to her place, really nice, lots of rooms, and quiet, nobody else around."

Johnny Belmont paused to slurp his drink and poke Jack in the chest. "You listening?"

Jack figured he'd better let Johnny Belmont think that he was a friend before he tried to get any info out of him, so he said, "Sure, I'm listening."

Johnny Belmont sniffed hard before going on. "So she takes me into her bedroom, crazy man, it's like Marie Antoinette's bood-wah or something, know what I mean? Like chandeliers, and this huge bed with a canopy, and oriental rugs, paintings on the walls, the whole thing, and she goes, 'Take off your clothes, I'll be right back' and she goes into the bathroom, so I strip off my clothes, but I leave my socks on, and I'm feeling kind of stupid, 'cause I'm like . . . hard, you know? I'm sporting wood, like a full-on throbbing chubby, so I like sit down on the bed, and she's got fur sheets, I mean, fucking fur sheets!"

Johnny Belmont paused, expecting an amazed response. Mac looked evenly at the glass he was drying. Jack didn't know what to say, so he said nothing.

Johnny Belmont looked back and forth at them. "Yeah. Like you guys fuck on fur sheets every night! Jeez! Do you hear me? *Fur sheets!—snort—*So I'm sitting there sliding around on those fur sheets, tickling my ass, and like the back of my sack, you know? I love that shit. So I'm just waiting, and I want to grab it but I can't, you know, so I'm like trying to think of stuff that'll make me deflate, like fucking Buddy Hackett or somebody, you know what I mean? But it ain't working, but it doesn't matter, cause she comes back out, and she's got on this crazy negligée that's like split in the crotch, and her nipples are springing out, and it's all like green lace and satin and whatnot, and she's so fucking hot, and I'm sitting there on the edge of the bed, and she starts licking me, I mean slowly up the sides and around the top, and I'm like about to spout and she knows it, and she's like, she goes 'Hold on there, it's my turn!' and she gets in the bed, leaning up against the pillows, and she spreads her legs and starts petting herself, and she goes, 'Come here, kneel in front of me, put your face here, come here,' so I do what she says, and I think she wants me to lick her but she goes,

'Don't touch, just watch. Just watch what happens now!'
And she gets my arms in this fucking judo hold and a guy in
a Batman suit jumps out of the armoire! He's got this
Batman suit on, fucking mask and ears and utility belt and
everything, except his dick is sticking out, and it's huge! And
I'm looking at him over my shoulder, but I can't move,
'cause she's got me in this judo hold, and Batman comes up
behind me and starts fucking me up the ass! He just starts
banging me, fucking my ass, and I'm screaming!—*snort*—
I'm screaming, 'What the fuck? Fuck you, Batman! Get the
fuck out of my ass!' I'm screaming and she's laughing and
she lets go of me and starts working herself, her pussy is
right in my face, and she's masturbating and screaming, 'Yes!
Fuck him, Batman! Go Batman! Fuck his ass!' And I'm
screaming, 'Fuck you, Batman!' And he's just banging away
at my ass, and she's shrieking, 'Yes! Yes!' And getting off, her
pussy is right there in my face, and my ass is like splitting in
two, it's killing me, he's huge, and right up in there, I thought
it would tear in half. And now I'm just screaming 'Help! No!
No more! Get offa me!' And she's like 'Yes! Yes! Come
Batman! Come' And Batman pulls out of my ass, and it's like
spasming, I mean like I just shat Batman, you know what I
mean? It's like throbbing and burning and Batman just
shoots all over me, it's a fucking full-on Batgasm, and it goes
all over my back and onto her stomach and face, and she's
screaming, I mean, she's just freaking out, she's getting off so
hard, and I'm in agony and like covered in Batman's cum,
and he's fucking laughing, and she's laughing, and they
throw me on the floor and stuff my head in a pillowcase, and
I'm in so much pain, and they throw me in a car, and by the

time I get the pillow case offa my head, we're on the FDR, and the driver goes, 'Where to?' And I'm like 'Fuck you man, let me off here,' so he gets off the FDR at Houston and leaves me at Avenue D and I walk home. I walk all the way home with a pillowcase tied around my throbbing ass."

Johnny Belmont sat back, snorted loudly, and took a gulp from his drink. No one said anything for a moment.

"I think you already told me that story," Mac mused, "Or somebody did. I know I've heard the Batman story before."

"Well then he's done it before! I'm sure he has. I'm sure this wasn't the first time she took somebody home from here so Batman could fuck him up the ass."

Mac was summoned by a patron at the other end of the bar, and was glad to get away. Johnny Belmont drained his beer and slammed the glass down in triumph.

Jack finished his beer slowly to buy a minute to plan his move. He had to gain the advantage. While Mac circled back and refilled their glasses, Jack slid a business card under the cellophane wrapper on a pack of Seaweeds and placed it carefully on the bar between puddles. Johnny Belmont noticed it, then jumped back in alarm when its implications became clear.

"Fuck . . . fuck that! You're with *them*? Then fuck you! No way. Landis ruined me! Talk about fucking me up the ass. Jeez!"

Jack narrowed his eyes. "I don't know about that," he said. "They tell me that before you could completely ruin yourself, Landis saved you."

"Is that what they tell you? Did they also tell you that we're square? Because we are. Johnny Belmont don't have debts.

Johnny Belmont don't owe Landis anything. Johnny Belmont did everything they asked, and that's it. Over. Done. Johnny Belmont is off the hook, right? Did they tell you that?"

"They told me that Johnny Belmont worked with Victor Sargasso a while ago."

"Yeah, so? Sure, I worked with Victor. Great guy. Lousy card player. So what?"

"So—maybe you know where he is now."

Johnny Belmont nodded in realization. "That what this is about? How the fuck should I know? I haven't seen him. It's been years. No idea. OK? We're done? Good to meet you . . . er," Johnny Belmont read Jack's card. "Jack Fish. Haw! That's good! I haven't seen Victor since I don't know when, 'K? Bye."

Johnny Belmont got off his stool, pocketed the smokes, and turned for the door.

Quickly, Jack grabbed Johnny Belmont by the arm. "You help me find Victor, and Landis forgets about the twenty thousand dollars."

Belmont whirled around. "The twenty thou? Fuck you! Those were legitimate expenses!"

"Maybe they were, and maybe they weren't." Jack unfolded the "receipt" for his Chinese food. "The managers at Landis think that a massage parlour in Jackson Heights may not have had very much to do with your business with Victor Sargasso."

"That place was crucial! Absolutely strategic!"

"I think I'll go check it out then. And the Tubby Jockey Social Club. Because as I'm sure they told you, it's not a good idea to owe the Pool Supply people money for very long, is it?"

"Are you threatening me?"

"Yes, I am."

"Jeez."

"Look, Landis isn't asking very much of you this time. In fact, it's a pretty good deal—twenty thousand dollars for one piece of information. Where is Victor Sargasso?"

Johnny Belmont sat back down on his stool. He sniffed heavily, rubbed his nose and said, "So that's how they play it. I should've known."

"How's that?"

"They wait. Patient-like. I thought I was clear. Five, six years, nobody says nothing, I figured they'd let me have the twenty. Should've known."

"Landis has a long memory."

"Buy me another drink."

Jack signaled to Mac who set them up again. Jack laid down two fives and nodded to the Scotsman who gave the bar a cursory wipe with his soiled rag and moved on.

Belmont said, "Fucking aggressive pool suppliers, aren't you? Who the hell are you guys really?"

Jack laughed. "Very competitive business, pool supplies."

After a minute of thoughtful drinking, Johnny Belmont admitted, "Look, I don't have any idea where Victor is. But I know someone who might."

"Who?"

"Victor used to be with this artist chick. Freaky bitch. Does this fucked-up performance crap. I have no idea what it's about, but it's great to watch, she always gets naked and her tits are like rockets. I don't think they're still together. But she might know where he is now. And she's easy to find."

"How? Where?"

"She's always performing somewhere. I'll find out, call you tomorrow, 'K?"

"Landis wants Victor Sargasso back. If I don't bring him in, they want me to take you diving. Without a snorkle. You understand?"

"I'll call you tomorrow."

"The number is on the card."

Johnny Belmont tipped his pint back and swallowed the dregs of his umpteenth beer of the night. He waved to Mac, mock-saluted Jack, and shoved off for the dark, dirty and cold room in Hell's Kitchen he called home.

Jack was exhausted. His first extended effort at spycraft, his first full day of breathing and the flow of beer down his gullet combined to overwhelm. He put his head down on the bar and closed his eyes, just for a minute.

Hours later, he awoke, freezing and wet on the kitchen floor in the safehouse. He had no idea how he'd gotten there, whether he'd been guided by Poseidon or a posse of phantom lobsters. Jack filled the tub and removed his clothes. He slipped under the warm water and went back to sleep. He dreamt about the pet dogfish he had as a kid.

The Abyss was on HBO. Jack assumed it was a comedy and was having a good laugh when the phone rang.

"I'll pick you up in an hour."

"Johnny?"

"Do me a favor, OK? Don't use my name on the telephone. And don't ever call me Johnny, OK? It's Johnny Belmont. You ready to go?"

"Where are we going?"

"The Chloe Mitosis show is tonight. I said I'd take you, right? So Johnny Belmont is taking you."

"Good. Yes. An hour?"

"Where are you?"

Jack started to give the address of the safehouse, then

thought better of it. "I'll be in front of the L stop on Bedford."

"Brooklyn? Figures. OK. And remember. I take you to Chloe, that erases my debt."

"I never agreed to that. . ." but Johnny Belmont didn't hear him because he'd already hung up.

Two hours later, Jack was leaning against a pay phone on the corner of Bedford and North Seventh, nursing an I ♥ NY paper cup of coffee as he watched the parade emerging from the subway—quasi-hipsters returning from work, and even less cool Manhattanites slumming the boroughs, looking for the New Thing which somebody told them was now out here. The Poles and Italians, who had always been in the neighborhood, flowed around them, heading home to wives and husbands and kids and hearty dinners and American TV.

Jack was looking the wrong way when a decommissioned Crown Vic pulled up in front of him. A bright light shone in his face as Johnny Belmont's voice, compressed and amplified through the PA horn in the grill, barked, "Jack Fish! Get in the vehicle. Now!"

Passersby gave him a wide berth as Jack opened the door. The car accelerated with a shriek from the rear tires before he was all the way inside.

"Ha! You can take Johnny Belmont out of the police, but you can't take the police out of Johnny Belmont!"

Johnny Belmont may not have been a cop anymore, but he still drove like one. He barely paused at red lights, tailgated

slower cars and forced them to pull over with a flash of his
brights and a squawk from his illegal siren. Jack could tell
that he was generally going in a direction opposite the one
Dick had driven when he chauffeured Jack into
Williamsburg. Belmont followed the river for a while until
he got to the Navy Yard. Then, instead of getting onto the
highway, Belmont took the street under it. It was a dicey
netherworld of massive, windowless self-storage warehouses and the rusty pylons and girders that supported the
BQE. The street itself was an obstacle course of gaping sink
holes, dead mufflers, shed bumpers, bags of used diapers,
and dazed-looking people wielding squeegees and cups of
change as they wandered among the cars bottled up near
the on-ramps to the Expressway. Trucks snorted and rat-
tled and rumbled overhead.

"Here," Johnny Belmont said, both hands letting go of
the steering wheel. "Steer!"

Without waiting for Jack to grip the wheel, Belmont
reached under the seat and pulled out a Te Amo cigar box.
He opened it, perused the contents, and selected a small foil
packet and a short straw. He offered the open box to Jack.
"Need anything?"

Jack was too concerned with watching the road to look
down. "I'm fine," he said, wrenching the wheel hard to
maneuver around a garbage can stuck halfway down a deep
pothole.

Johnny Belmont closed the box, spread out the foil on the
lid and leaned in for a loud toot. His right foot stepped heavily on the accelerator and the Crown Vic picked up speed,
the steering wheel skittering like a live eel in Jack's hand.

Johnny Belmont lifted his head up, tucked the box away, and retook the wheel. Jack wasn't sure if they were any safer.

When Belmont ran a light and nearly plowed into the side of an actual police car, Jack expected to be arrested, if not shot, on the spot. But all Johnny Belmont did was wave to the other driver, raising the fingers on his driving hand without removing his thumb from the steering wheel. The cop in the cruiser returned the gesture.

"That's Garcia. Good guy. Got a little smack problem, but we all have our weaknesses, don't we?" Belmont smiled at Jack and poked himself in the chest. "And mine would have to be the ladies!"

Johnny Belmont and Jack cruised through the nighttime-quiet streets of the daytime-hectic Downtown Brooklyn, past somber buildings that supplied government, discount athletic footwear, and fried chicken to the borough—the family courts and V.I.M. and Borough Hall and Dr. Jay's and Kennedy and the State Supreme Court and Popeyes and Modell's and Luthur's. And Johnny Belmont never stopped talking: about the ladies, about chicks, about girls, about broads, sluts, slashes, gashes, Bettys, bitches, mamas, Veronicas, chiquitas, lezbos, foxes, snatches, hos and women.

"That's my hangup!" Belmont said. "Pussy! Hey—you know what all that stuff around a vagina is called?"

Jack tried to ignore the question. He wished his mission was to kill Belmont, not Sargasso. He tried to pay attention to the great stone footing of the Brooklyn Bridge as they drove down to Fulton Landing.

"A woman!" Johnny Belmont cackled.

Jack grimaced in disgust and pulled a newspaper off the

dashboard. As he scanned the page, the name *Chloe Mitosis* jumped out of a caption and caught his eye. It was a review in an old copy of the Arts and Leisure section of the *Times*:

> . . . her naked body covered in squid ink squeezed from a living animal pulled fresh from a tank. I was intrigued, then appalled, when she proceeded to vomit in rainbow colors and then roll around screaming on the floor, which had been papered with posters of the Olsen twins. While her work is certainly provocative, the question I am left asking myself after the performance is not 'is it art?' but 'why do I have to keep watching this stuff?'

"Like I said," said Johnny Belmont as he tapped the picture. "She's got rack *and* back!"

The public pool building had been grand and condescending once, like a library or a post office in the great city-as-noble-service-provider tradition. Now it was a graffiti-covered shell throbbing with light and sound, surrounded by a much-breached chain-link fence. Jack could smell the chlorine and the bleach, the sweat and the pot smoke billowing out through the holes in the roof, pouring down the crumbling brick walls, cascading down the shattered flight of shallow concrete steps to dissipate into the murk of the neighborhood. Skateboarders were tumbling down the stairs, attempting ollies and grab-tricks, and mostly landing on their asses as their boards clattered toward the arriving throngs.

Jack and Johnny Belmont followed two very tall and bored-looking women and their shared, bored and blond-bearded consort in leather culottes through a hole in the fence, up the stairs, through the turnstile and inside where they were frisked for weapons before being allowed to join the party.

Johnny Belmont led Jack into a semicircular room packed with people. It functioned as an antechamber to the locker rooms, and it had suffered a long decline. The glass was gone from the high skylights, the trophy cases had been looted and stood broken and empty, and the WPA frescoes were waterstained and crumbling, peeling away in chunks that fell to the terrazzo floor. The murals depicted the happy, swimming workers of Depression-era Brooklyn, frolicking in the pools. They were workers who made things. Big, true things like boilers and smelters and girders and ships and tanks and church steeples and bridges—things that required boilers and smelters and girders as well as huge, rippling muscles on wide, sturdy frames, and a strong brotherly communal workers' spirit to make. The people in the frescoes had imposing physiques, square shoulders, bronze skin, and clear eyes, sharpened with a sense of purpose. They made things that people needed and that would last for centuries. The work they did was for the good of the common man. It was tough and honest, like them.

Jack noticed that the people at the party looked nothing like the people in the murals. These were the new workers of Brooklyn. The work they did was casual, freelance, consulting or "independent contracting." They made things like PowerPoint presentations and intranets and "solutions" to non-existent problems, things that required frustrating computers running shoddy software to make things that nobody really wanted and that had no permanence or truth, things that would soon be obsolete and forgotten. Many were "between jobs" and seeking inspiration through chemicals and sex and having brunch a lot, even on weekdays. They were pale, thin, fragile, sickly, pasty, dirty, skinny caffeine-addicted American Spirit-smoking vegetarians, and their eyes were glazed over from boredom, from CRT burnout, from fluorescent lighting, from reading the subtitles on foreign films, from reading poetry on the subway, from squinting in disgust at people who fit in established social groups and had money and comfort and didn't conceive of a status quo as something to struggle against. And they were ready to party in their own disaffected weird way.

Johnny Belmont pointed at the woman tending a makeshift bar and said, "She's Chloe Mitosis. OK? You talk to her, she'll tell ya where Sargasso is—*sniff*—that's the best I can do, OK? I'll be around, you let me know how it goes. Believe me, I wish I could do more, but, y'know?" and he slapped Jack on the shoulder and slipped away, eyes on the foil-wrapped ass of a hand model from Mali.

Chloe. She was tall, severe, with pale skin and spikey, artificially white hair and a steel stud sticking out of her face between her lower lip and her chin. She was wearing a black halter top with the words SUPER POOPER screened on the chest, tight black jeans, big black boots, and a studded belt. She was tending the diving-board bar that was set up on deck chairs. Jack sidled up to what would be the bouncy end and leaned in with his palms down on the gritty no-slip surface. Chloe was working the other end of the board. Jack's hands gravitated to a stack of promotional postcards and slid the top one off. The glossy side held an image of a woman—Chloe, Jack realized—wearing nothing but what looked like blocks of blue ice around her biceps and thighs, and a hat of flames. She held a red lollipop in her left hand and a blue one in her right. He flipped the card over and read the title, I BLOW HOT AND COLD, and the address, CHLOE MITOSIS STUDIO B21, 1205 MANHATTAN AVE AT THE END OF BROOKLYN 11211.

"WhatcanIgetcha?" Chloe asked, still pouring a blue-green cocktail from a chrome shaker with her left hand and opening a Rolling Rock with her right.

"What's that?" Jack pointed to the cocktail.

"House drink. Called the Deep End—High Tide Gatorade, cheap vodka, Midori, and a shot of chlorine. Fucks you up *and* replenishes your electrolytes. Costs extra for me to pee in it—*wink*—It's terrible. Have a beer instead."

He heard her, but was curious. "No, gimme one of those."

She shrugged, shook up another Deep End and poured it, all the while popping the tops off Rocks and setting up tequila shots for the hands clutching money that came reaching over the diving board.

She pushed the cocktail to Jack and said, "Six bucks."

Jack pulled a fistful of his fives from his pocket and handed Chloe two of them, which she stuffed in her pants without making change.

"Drink up," she said, laughing at him with her eyes.

Jack toasted her with his glass and took a sip. It was like swallowing used pool water. He soured his mouth at the Deep End.

Chloe snorted and took a long look at Jack. She leaned in over the diving board.

"Told ya to have a beer. So what's up with you? This isn't your crowd. How'd you get in to this thing?"

"Right." Jack figured it was the moment to get down to business. He leaned in until their faces were close—Chloe's features lit aqua from the light filtering through his drink.

Jack tried his suave, spy-in-the-know voice, "I'm an old friend of Victor Sargasso's. We used to work together. Do you know where I can find him?"

Chloe pushed back from Jack a bit and eyed at him suspiciously. She said robotically, "Victor. No. It's been a long time. I don't have any idea where he is now."

"Oh," said Jack. His thoughts jumped to getting better info out of Johnny Belmont.

"But if I do run into him, who should I say is looking for him?" Chloe was staring hard at Jack. Her voice had lost all playfulness and had become hostile.

Jack dug out a card and passed it to her. "It's kind of funny," he said, glancing around, "what with me being in the pool supply business and all . . ."

She read it and quickly suppressed a look of alarm. "Yeah, well, like I said, I haven't seen him. Now, if you'll excuse me, I've got work to do. Stick around for the show. No. On second thought, don't."

Chloe moved to the other end of the diving board to sell E and Sunny D to some fifteen-year-olds. Jack tried another sip of his chlorine cocktail, certain that he had screwed up the encounter with Chloe. She had something she wasn't giving up.

"Where ya from? Definitely not New York—somewhere

else, right?" The question came from a skinny girl wearing a TRUCKING FOR JESUS hat, a tankini and flip-flops. One of those people who wrongly decided that since Brooklyn wasn't in Manhattan it was in the Midwest. One of those people the City should have mugged and sent home, but never did. Blond hair in two braids came down from either side of her hat, and freckles dotted her cheeks and retroussé nose.

Annoyed with himself for his clumsy spycraft, Jack laced his words with sarcasm and spat, "Somewhere else, yeah. Atlantis, actually."

"Eeew. I hate Atlanta. It's like L.A. without the beach or good-looking people, right? Ugh. Atlanta. I had to spend five months there on a movie for Cinemax. Fuckin' Larry Dingle wouldn't leave his trailer unless someone wiped him first—yuck."

"I didn't say Atlanta. I said—"

"Don't try to back out of it now, Georgia-boy! Just because I'm dissing your town. I know. You're going to tell me how friendly it is. Peachtree Boulevard. Southern Hospitality. Chicken-fried steak. I mean, what the hell is that? If it wasn't for the Waffle House, I'd have gone crazy—love them pancakes! Come with me, I've got some kind in my locker."

"I didn't say—"

"Bored now!" She pulled his arm. "Let's go." And she marched him into the locker room on the left, where the sign used to say LADIES and now said BREEDERS, to differentiate it from the locker room on the right, FAGS AND DYKES.

The atmosphere in the Breeders' locker room was warm, moist, and charged, throbbing with drum-and-bass breakbeats and yellow-tinged emergency lights glowing and dimming on a cycle. Art was hanging above the lockers on the walls, panoramic photographs of quintessential American vistas like Half Dome and Mount Rushmore, with people having sex in the foreground. LANDSCAPE PORNOGRAPHY read the title card for the exhibit. Jack was particularly struck by a huge print of a woman getting rimmed on the rim of the Grand Canyon.

The lockers themselves were battered and rusty, arrayed around the perimeter of the large, square room. There were benches in the middle, facing the lockers, with people on them, and other people on top of some of the people, moving, laughing, moaning. Jack saw Johnny Belmont working a Puerto Rican girl who had her hands on her hips, her foot out sideways, and was tipping her head back and forth in the international sign for "I'm *not* trying to hear that."

Trucking for Jesus led Jack to a locker in the middle of a row, spun the combo lock, and pulled it open with a shudder and a squeak. She reached for an Altoids tin on the top shelf, opened it, extracted a small pipe and a lighter, sparked it up, took a deep drag off the pipe, and passed it to Jack, eyes half closed, head back, exhaling as little as possible when she said, "You gonna swim in that outfit?"

"What? This? Um. No . . ." Jack held the hot pipe gingerly between thumb and forefinger. She handed him the lighter and he followed her example. He held the pipe to his lips, lit the lighter, smelled his eyebrow burning, coughed through the pipe, and watched the bowlful of glowing weed shoot out of the pipe, arc through the air, and sizzle to black mush on the wet floor. Trucking for Jesus snorted out a cloud of sweet smoke as a huge laugh burst from her.

"If I paid for that shit, I'd be pissed. Hang on . . ." She poked around in the tin, came up with a tablet, shoved it in Jack's mouth, and put her hand to his lips until he swallowed.

"That should be more your speed."

"Speed?"

She gave Jack an incredulous look. "Why would I give you speed? Let's go for a swim."

Almost immediately, Jack stood resplendent in his mankini, the rest of his clothes balled up and jammed in an unlocked locker he would never find again. Trucking for Jesus led him through the gauntlet of mandatory showers—alternating temperature extremes, freezing cold, then scalding hot, then freezing cold, then scalding hot. Jack passed through the last sequence, gasping hard as his skin tightened all over and his heart closed shut for an uncomfortably long time, then screamed out as he was scalded and jolted into fluttery arhythmia. Then he was outside, in the night, in the walled-in euphoria of the pools: the warm, shallow kiddie pool, the drained and dismantled diving pool, and the vast, green, algae-thick main pool.

A group of men circled the kiddie pool, urinating into the low water like putti. Jack wasn't sure if they were making ironic artistic kiddie-pool commentary, or if they were just a bunch of drunk, selfish, partying men peeing into a pool. Not having to go himself, Jack moved on to the diving pool, which contained no water but was far from empty.

The dry pool floor was painted with a grid of large black dots over which a tangled mass of mostly naked people were clumped. A man sat on the diving board platform, dangling his feet over the edge where the board had been removed to make the bar inside. He had a smear of zinc oxide cream on his nose and a whistle on a string around his neck that he blew before spinning a spinner and shouting, "Left hand black!" through a megaphone. The semi-naked clump struggled and shifted, and a topless woman flopped on the ground jiggling and giggling and out of the game. Fascinated, Jack sat down on a deck chair. The whistle blew again, the spinner spun, and the man with the white nose called out, "Right foot black!" The pile groaned and stretched and partially collapsed, losing about half its members to the floor. The ones who remained laughed and pushed and fought to maintain position. Muscle and sinew stretched taut, flesh glistened and slid, the whistle blew, the spinner spun.

Trucking for Jesus sat next to Jack. "Dude, after this game, Chloe Mitosis is gonna do her thing in there."

Jack perked up. "Her thing? What's her thing?"

"No way! You've never seen her perform? Just wait!"

There were three people left in the Black Twister game, two women and a man, and when the whistle blew and "Left foot black" was called again, they tumbled and lay sprawled and gasping. The spinner man climbed down from his platform. The game was over.

Trucking for Jesus sat up tall in her chair. "Yeah, OK. Here we go. Check this out. Here she comes."

The crowd knew it, too. They gathered around the pool and smoked quietly, waiting for something to happen.

With a whiney blast of bagpipes from the sound system, six rippling pallbearers emerged from the Fags and Dykes locker room wearing bow ties, vests, and satin pants, carrying two surfboards supporting a giant clam. They walked in somber lockstep to the empty pool and down wooden planks to its concrete bottom. They lowered the surfboards and placed them on the pool floor, then returned to the locker room. The DJ went wild, cross fading "Octopus's Garden" with Rick James and Steve Reich while a bald, naked, and very muscular man covered in paprika wheeled a pink Styrofoam cooler on a red Radio Flyer wagon to the base of the high dive. He sprang up the ladder using only his feet, winched the cooler up, and took his position on the diving platform. The six pallbearers had returned, now dressed as firemen and dragging heavy hoses. A troupe of Taiko drummers perched around the pool set up a languorous beat that slowly, inexorably built upon itself. The pallbearers-turned-fireman turned their sudsy nozzles on the clam and lavished the pool with foaming jets of water.

Paprika Man removed the lid from his cooler and began lobbing chunks of dry ice that popped and burst into vapor when they hit the gathering water. The clam rose steadily, majestically on the surge, amid white puffs and billows and streamers. The drums built and built and built. Paprika Man hurled his last chunk of dry ice as the drums peaked. The firemen shut off their hoses; the water and the clam had reached the lip of the pool. A spotlight knifed through the party and burned on the clam. The drumming ceased. The clam opened. It was filled with translucent goo that covered a large, pink pearl. The pearl moved, uncurled, wobbled and finally stood. It was Chloe—coated, viscous, dripping, glorious, naked, primordial, and enraged. She glared and howled—one syllable, one word, one cry of power, of denial, of negation—

"Noooooooooooooooooooooooooooooooooooooooooooo!"

—as she swept her gaze back and forth across the crowd. Wherever it fell, it chilled with cold, dark energy. She froze the party, then collapsed into the gooey clam.

The firemen turned their jets on Chloe, blasting the sticky sheet off her skin in curds and pushing the clam/surfboard raft beneath the diving platform. Paprika Man, who had begun to yodel in the alpine style, jumped from the platform, turning in the air above the clam in a lazy flip that didn't quite complete. He splashed down flat on his back with a sickening *thwack*, sending a gasp and an empathetic "ooh" through the crowd. The firemen now turned their hoses on him, dissolving his powdery coat into a vermillion stain that spread outward from his point of impact. Chloe let out another primal wail, leapt from her clam and landed on the floating man's chest, standing on her feet. A lone cowboy wearing a ten-gallon hat, Roper boots, and assless chaps came trotting out of the homo locker room on a mule. With a "Yip!" and a "Hee-ya!" he lassoed Chloe around the waist and pulled her, still balanced atop Paprika Man, to the shallow end of the pool. Amid tremendous applause and renewed pounding by the Taiko drummers, Chloe hopped off Paprika Man onto the dry concrete, leaving his greasy body bobbing lifelessly in the red water. She vaulted onto the back of the mule. The cowboy kicked its flanks and—*clippity clop*—they rode toward the locker rooms.

The show was over.

The DJ spun a mash-up of "I'm Too Sexy," Mozart's *Requiem*, and "Caroline Says."

Jack was stunned. What did it mean? How did she think it up? How long had she practiced surfing on a slippery bald man? He leapt to his feet, clapping and cheering. That's when the pill kicked in.

His vision blurred, his skin felt warm and furry, his breathing came to a grinding halt. Landsick, but worse. Trucking for Jesus licked Jack's cheek and murmured a list of sexual positions into his ear, but he pushed her aside.

"Tentacles," he croaked and staggered through the uneven rows of deck chairs and towels, picnics, and people going at it. He reached the edge of the largest pool with its thrashing crowd and greenish water, and plunged in headfirst, arms at his side, barely disturbing the thick surface tension.

The water was stagnant, oxygen-heavy on top, and choked with algae. Still, it was welcome, wet succor to Jack. He swam the perimeter staying about a foot above the chunky bottom, slipping past slippery legs and round butts as new revelers leapt overhead and plunged into the swampy throng with squeals and concussive *plops*.

The drugs and the wet and the oxygen and the exhaustion reached chemical equilibrium inside Jack, and Jack reached physical equilibrium in the pool, subconsciously, metabolically controlling his buoyancy to remain halfway between the slick surface and the littered bottom. There, he swallowed his tongue, rolled his eyes back into his head, and attempted to grok the fullness of Chloe's performance.

It took a while, in the drug-addled muck and echoing sexy

chaos, but the swimmers gradually became aware of the flotsam that was Jack in their midst.

"Oh my God!"

"There's some dude—"

"Freakin' corpse in the pool—"

"Oh shit, another floater!"

"Get him out!"

"Eeew!"

"Oh my God!"

"No, pull his arms . . . his arms!"

"Get your hands in his armpits—"

"What's that thing he's wearing?"

"Take his legs—"

"My God! How much water did he soak up?"

"Fucker weighs a ton!"

"Is he breathing?"

"We should get a *real* lifeguard next time!"

"Oh my God!"

"Put him on his back—"

"Turn his head to the side—"

"Christ! Half the pool is pouring out of him!"

"Where is his tongue?"

"Oh my God!"

"Does he have a heartbeat?"

"Oh, for fuck's sake, get out of the way!"

Jack's eyes rolled forward when he felt another mouth on his. He unswallowed his tongue and gently probed the other mouth with it, adding a little suction as the other mouth blew life-giving air into him. The other mouth broke free of his and cut off the life-giving air immediately, and a hand slapped him hard. He opened his eyes to see to whom the mouth and slap belonged—Chloe.

"Fucking asshole! What the fuck, you stupid fuck—"

Jack put his mouth back on hers to stop the flow of fucks. He reached up and pulled her down to him. She was sticky from the goo, and overheated from her performance, and furious with Landis and its employees, and instead of pushing away from him, she fell to Jack, and they started to roll, over and over, across the concrete, over the edge and into the pool. They slipped through the turgid surface, and now it was Jack who gave Chloe life, gently and continuously, as she wrapped her legs around him and his mankini sank to the littered bottom, never to be seen again.

Jack was sitting on his back on the Tüshî, polishing off the cold Moo Shu for breakfast, watching TV. He flipped channels from *20,000 Leagues Under the Sea* to *Atlantis Inferno*, but saw only the encounter with Chloe. It played repeatedly in his head—mostly the sex-in-the-pool part, but also the exchange at the diving board bar. He was sure that he had screwed it up. *She's hiding something,* he thought. *I should have been patient, should have gotten her to trust me more, I rushed it.*

But when? When was the crucial moment? Chloe had been suspicious to begin with, but something had shut her down completely. *The card!* Jack jumped up off the sofa. *Where was her studio?* Manhattan Avenue. Where in Hades was that? Jack stomped around the room, pulling open drawers and rifling through take-out menus. There was a phonebook under the telephone, and when Jack thumbed through it, a folded map fell out. He opened it. It was printed on pulpy paper with cheap inks that bled to near-illegibility. Jack held the map a few inches from his face to keep the tiny street names in focus, and scanned. He squinted back a headache. There. He'd found it. Manhattan Avenue ran up the spine of Greenpoint, and at the end, at the very tip of the borough, was something called the Newtown Creek, a slash of a canal that fed into the East River. It wasn't far away. Jack checked the mini subway map magnet on the fridge, and shook his head. Even in Atlantis, everybody knew the G train was the worst. It would be faster to swim. Safer, too—easier to evade the Maltese underwater.

Jack rummaged around in the kitchen drawers until he found what he wanted—a gallon-size Ziploc bag, which he stowed in his backpack. Then he left the apartment and walked circuitously down to the park by the river, where Dick had dropped him off. He was sure he hadn't been followed. The early afternoon sun smoldered in the hazy sky over lower Manhattan. He walked past a brick smokestack, all that remained from the molasses factory that had once stood there, and found that he wasn't alone.

A pair of toothless fishermen sat on the shattered rocks of the riverbank, with bagged forties beside them. They nodded to Jack as he took off his clothing and stuffed it into the Ziploc, squeezing the air out and zipping it closed. Naked, except for his Mets backpack, he stood on a slimy rock sunk in the mud at the water's edge and looked out at the river. Muscular, blind, and at odds with itself, so full of the influence of larger, more noble bodies of water—the Harbor, the Hudson, the Sound—the East River could only assert its identity through rage and hate. It ran upstream and downstream simultaneously, trying and failing to hold the tide from the sea and the flow from the Adirondacks in its knotty grasp. Jack could smell its self-loathing and its violence.

"I wouldn't be swimmun' in there, no way, no how," said one of the fishermen. The other pursed his lips and spat through his rotten gums.

Jack dove in, careful to avoid their baited hooks and the gray steel pipes that extended underwater from the oil refinery. Immediately, the river knew he was there and pulled him down to its sticky bottom in a coil of current. Jack didn't fight it. The river was in constant motion, flowing in every possible direction, and Jack let it carry him toward his destination. Like a salmon fighting its way upstream, he slalomed against the main flow, using the river's twists and eddies to sling himself along. His route wasn't direct, but Jack had a goal—and he would get there.

He moved through the river, sliding in graceful curves and diagonals through its turbid geometry. It felt good to be able to move this way again, breaking out of the flat plain of limited movement afforded by the surface. When his way forward was blocked or he was hemmed in on the sides, Jack danced up or down, spinning, tumbling, spearing through the murk until he was carried past, around, or through each submarine obstacle.

Visibility was so poor, Jack often hit things before he could see what they were. Impenetrably cloudy with particles of sludge and soot and grime and mud, the river hurled

Jack into sunken shopping carts and tree limbs and chemical drums and tangled knots of cable. The blown safes and weighted canvas sacks and cars and boots and guns seemed to be most crowded near the bank, so Jack wormed his way around a sunken pier to the middle of the river. There he had other problems—the deeper water flowed more determinedly downstream toward the sea, and the surface was crowded with traffic. The parade of pleasure boats, NYPD harbor cruisers, Coast Guard vessels, tugs, tankers, ferries, and the Circle Line, all threatened to shred Jack with a propeller or bludgeon him with a rusty metal hull. He veered back toward the Brooklyn shore, preferring the steady but less lethal battering of shopping carts to the risk of sudden death by tugboat. A gang of Striped Bass eyed him coolly, and kept swimming. Jack made sure to stay out of their way.

Somewhere along the Northside-Greenpoint border, Jack surfaced under a partially collapsed dock. He gauged his progress against the four smokestacks of the power plant across the water on Avenue D. Overhead, helicopters whupped through the air. Leviathan Manhattan teemed with traffic and commerce and self-importance, just far enough away to seem remote and glorious and imaginary. Wavelets slapped against the dock's concrete pilings, which the bitter river had eroded, exposing the rusting rebar inside. Jack could see a confluence ahead, where the river swelled and bent. There he would find his way into the Newtown Creek. He let himself sink and resumed his dance upstream.

When he felt a warm, oily surge from his right, Jack knew he had arrived. The Newtown Creek poured its saccharine, chemical-laced current into the East River's turmoil, creating a series of whirlpools and standing waves shiny with hydro-carbons and petrochemicals and liquefied garbage. Jack swam against the flow and into the maw of pollution. His eyes burned as he searched for a way up and out, and he nearly sank before he found it: the rotten rungs of a ladder nailed into the creosote-soaked bulkhead that fixed the creek's southern banks in a black wall of tar.

Dripping with grimy water, Jack flopped onto a cracked concrete wharf and took shelter behind a van with cin-derblocks for wheels. He waited until he had dried off a bit and could breathe with some confidence. Then he removed the Ziploc from his wet backpack, took out his clothes and got dressed. His back to the brick wall of a massive factory, Jack couldn't be seen—except by the guy loading sheet metal onto a flatbed on the Queens side of the creek, and he was union, so he didn't care.

The red-brick complex was a relic of the Manufacturing Age, with its monolithic smokestack and sawtooth skylights and loading docks with wooden roll-up doors and immense drafty windows with chickenwire embedded in the glass. A century earlier, seven or eight buildings had been constructed and combined to make a massive rope mill, which had since been foreclosed, abandoned, torched, squatted, repossessed, and reborn. Jack went up a short flight of cement steps and entered the building through a heavy steel door propped open with an eight-inch cast iron valve.

He was in a hallway lined with bicycles locked to water pipes and metal banisters that ran up and down the creaky wooden stairs. A rack of irregular mailboxes was fixed to the wall next to a bulletin board posted with flyers and cards and the recycling schedule.

Jack heard footsteps and voices and he hurried into the labyrinth of drywall partitions that had been constructed by the artists and craftspeople who had taken over the building. They had subdivided the open floors into enormous spaces and then subdivided these into workshops and studios and ateliers, places true to the building's intended purpose: making stuff. Some of the identical gray steel doors that Jack passed stood open. He caught glimpses of huge monochromatic canvases, sprinting whippets stopped mid-stride with strobe photography, a full-sized replica of a 1967 Lotus Elan carved from a block of cheese. To give the long-gone jute twining machines the headroom they needed, the high ceilings were supported by massive exposed wood columns and beams. These allowed the tenants to build lofts to sleep in, or to create enormous sculptures out of auto parts or chicken bones. The narrow maple floorboards creaked as Jack attempted to walk with the purposeful attitude that he knew where he was going. Which he did not.

A dead-end left Jack at the open door of a custom Velcro dartboard fabricator. A second flight of stairs brought him to another hall of steel doors and creaky floors and yet another flight of stairs, which brought him to the offices of an alternative-energy consultant. A heavy, black steel fire door was held ajar by a weight and pulley system tied in to the building's alarm system. Jack squeezed through it into another building in the complex, which was identical to the first except that its doors were painted hunter green instead of battleship gray.

Two men rolling a bronze walrus on a dolly came toward him. Jack gave them a preemptive nod and they nodded back. The noise from the dolly's hard rubber wheels made more conversation impossible, to Jack's relief. As he tramped down halls buzzing with power tools and skilled labor, Jack began to decipher the numbering system on the doors. He deduced that he had to go down one floor and cross into Building B to find Chloe's studio.

The door to studio B17 was open, and as he walked by, Jack saw a troupe of actors in khaki pants taking turns saying, "I am Galileo Galilei!" and falling to the floor, while a small woman with a crazed look in her eye beat a drum. He hurried past and continued down the hall.

When he got to Chloe's door, it was closed. Jack saw light leaking out underneath and heard the bass from her stereo. He casually walked past and tried the door handle of the next studio. It opened. A man looked up from a huge canvas divided into a grid, each square silk-screened with a big toe painted a different color. Jack apologized for interrupting and closed the door as the man swore at him in Greek. He turned around and again passed Chloe's door, stopping this time at studio B19. He twisted the knob. It turned. The door swung open a few inches, and he slipped through.

When his eyes had adjusted to the darkness, Jack found himself in a menagerie of the impossible. A lamb with bat wings and the head of a vulture stood atop a stainless steel operating table; a kangaroo with a Great White's dorsal fin, ibyx antlers, and a third eye stared at him from across the room; rows of jars held fetal pigs suspended in formaldehyde, each with its own fabulous mutation—a cluster of rat tails, an aardvark's nose, the delicate wings of a dragonfly. Insect and animal parts (eyes, wings, legs, tails, beaks, teeth, fins, feathers, fur, ears, tongues, claws) were carefully arranged in glass cases on the shelves, organized by species and waiting for the mad taxidermist to join them in the terrible forms and shapes of his imagination.

Careful to avoid touching the beasts, Jack crossed the cramped room to the wall it shared with Chloe's studio. He put his ear against it. The angry complaints of Staten Island Youth chunked from her stereo. The resident artists hadn't spent more than absolutely necessary on construction materials; there was a single thin layer of sheetrock between the studios. A steady chant—*I am Galileo Galilei*—leaked in from B17. Jack climbed the shelves in the corner and carefully drove the blade of his Swiss Army knife into the wall. Then, using the mini-saw, he cut himself an eyehole.

Chloe's space was kept intentionally dark; she had hung blackout curtains over the windows. In lieu of natural light, the room was illuminated by a dozen thrift-store lamps that stood on tables crammed with other objects. There was too much stuff for Jack to look at and differentiate into specific things. Raw materials, like buckets of paint and wheels and stacks of lumber, shared shelf and floor space with toys and *objets d'art* and stereo equipment. Her large drafting table was half buried under papers and cards, sketches and notes, videotapes, CDs, drawings, paintings, poems, and photographs. The pile was lit by two candelabra that burned with a dozen open flames, despite the landlord's specific injunction against open flames, which Jack had seen posted by the mailboxes.

Women in serge swimwear swam in tight formation in an Esther Williams movie, playing silently on a television. Models for the giant clamshell that Jack recognized from Chloe's performance piece were heaped on a countertop like the aftermath of a clambake. Saturated color blow-ups—Chloe as Venus, as Prometheus with a giant bird pecking at her crotch, as Heracles flooding a stable of smooth-chested cowboys with whipped cream—were tacked to the walls.

Chloe sat on a tall stool, wearing boots and belt, black cargo pants, and a black T-shirt with holes at the back of the collar. She poked at a pink clay bust of a philosopher with a knitting needle while she talked on a cordless phone. Jack pressed his ear to the hole.

"That's right, P-L-A-Y-D-O-H P-L-A-T-O—Yeah. A Play-Doh Plato. I'll shoot a Polaroid of it . . . Right—that's the idea—Plato's Fun Factory. Or like, Plato's Fuzzy Pumper Barber Shop. Imagine that, yeah. Aristotle sitting in a barber's chair getting pumped by Plato. What? No, no, no, for the opening I'm doing the sacrifice, just like we talked about . . . What? This afternoon? Like today? What the fuck? You can't move it up—I'm not ready! I still have to find people, and the stilts aren't here yet—What? All right, all *right*. I can be there in like an hour. And thanks again. I really need the work . . . I know. Bye."

Jack pressed his eye back to the hole. A disturbing pattern emerged from the clutter: a five-pronged spear that had been spray-painted gold was drying on newspaper spread on the floor; a skein of ultramarine blue cloth lay next to a long, hooded robe of the same material; a golden bowl on the drafting table held down a woodblock print of a temple in which a herd of bulls roamed freely; a knee-high clay model of Poseidon holding a spouting blowfish and a trident stood on a tree stump.

Chloe moved the bowl, rolled up the drawing, and stuck it into a black plastic tube. She folded the robe and put it into a portfolio case, along with a black sketchbook. One by one, she switched off the vintage lamps.

Jack clambered down from his perch and stepped quietly across the room. He stood with his ear to the door, listening. Finally, he heard Chloe's door close and her footsteps over muffled chants of *Lord Father, I beseech you!* Jack opened the door a crack and waited until he saw Chloe hurry past, then he paused thirty seconds by mentally reciting "Terra's Basement," before he slipped out into the hall.

Chloe was ahead of him, walking quickly. She wore an overlarge pair of headphones that covered her ears and was jacked into a CD player in the pocket of her cargo pants. The strap of the tube was slung over her shoulder, the top even with her bright white hair. She walked to the beat of the KLF mix she liked to use as ambient music for the subway. By the time Jack exited the building she was across the ad hoc parking lot at the far end of the street, where Manhattan Avenue met the creek. Jack stayed about half a block behind her, scrambling around cars, trying to keep her in sight while keeping out of her sight. She walked straight along Ash Street, past the Housing Authority garage and the auto parts distributor. The air was potpourri-sweet with stray esters from the candle factory that crouched beneath the Pulaski Bridge. Chloe made for the flight of metal stairs attached to the side of the bridge as if it was an afterthought and then she started climbing, skirting the guy wearing the puffy down coat and self-made plastic diaper who was snoring on the first landing.

Jack ducked into the loading bay of the Crab King warehouse. Stacks of plastic bins chattered as the doomed invertebrates scratched and clawed at the walls of their portable prisons. Asian guys with long-ash cigarettes and pallet jacks moved whole colonies of crustaceans into refrigerated trucks bearing the crowned crab logo and sent them on their way to the black bean sauce, garlic and oil, or melted butter that would be their end. Jack slipped into the rows of bins and waited. If he tried to move too soon, Chloe would easily spot him from the stairs, so he hid until she gained the bridge. Risking a peek, Jack looked back up the street. A gold IROC Z28 with a red-and-white flag on its antenna sat idling at a hydrant. One of the men inside was talking on a cell phone, another was eating a porkchop from an aluminum tray. Jack stole a glance at the stairs—Chloe was at the top now—and he made his move. Jack walked as fast as he could without running. He was almost to the stairway when through the constant tire and engine noise from the bridge roadway, the clamor of forklifts and trucks on the block, and the Cantopop on the radio in the Crab King warehouse, he heard a car door slam behind him. He walked faster, and sprang up the stairs, skirting the guy wearing the puffy down coat and self-made plastic diaper who was snoring on the first landing. Jack looked over the banister and saw his pursuer—a guy in

two-piece gold velour fashion sweats, jacket unzipped to
reveal gold medallions nestled in a mat of thick chest hair—
hustling along Ash Street with a crossbow in his hands.
Crabs! Jack pressed on, ducking instinctively when he heard
a metallic clang above him. A steel-tipped dart bounced off
the bottom of the span and fell into a Department of
Transportation dumptruck parked in the lot below. Down on
Ash Street, the guy in the gold tracksuit was reloading. Jack
dashed for the bridge.

Uncelebrated in song or postcard, the Pulaski Bridge was
not an engineering marvel. It was a short, broad, strong,
iron-framed, tough working bridge. It rose from each bank
of the Newtown Creek in a long concrete arc. In the middle
were two anchorages supporting a metal span that could be
raised to allow a schooner or an oil tanker to pass underneath. This happened maybe twice a year. The Pulaski
Bridge connected New York's two hardest-working boroughs, and at the moment, it took Chloe from Greenpoint to
Long Island City because, like many people, she hated the G
enough to walk to Queens and take the 7 instead.

Jack saw Chloe's white hair reach the apex of the
bridge's span. He was afraid of losing her, but more afraid
of getting jumped by the Maltese foot soldier behind him.
There was a small viewing platform that occupied the
anchorage on the Brooklyn side of the metal drawbridge.
Jack ducked behind an oil drum that now served as a
garbage can. A man who had recently emigrated from
Poland, where he spent most of his time drinking cheap
vodka on bridges, was standing there, drinking cheap
vodka on the bridge. Jack made the international sign for

Sssh! extending a finger before pursed lips as he ducked
down out of sight. The Pole smiled and said nothing. Jack
waited, crouched down with his back to the steel drum. He
waited . . . waited . . . waited . . . and pounced! when he
saw gold velour legs. He grabbed a pair of knees with both
hands, slammed his head between a man's thighs, and then
stood up fast, lifting, yelling, backing up to the side of the
bridge and shoving the Maltese stalker upwards over his
head, over his back, over the rail. *Splash.*

The Pole took a long swig from his GEOЯGI bottle and
offered it to Jack, who shook his head and ran.

Being this high over the water made Jack queasy, but he
forced his feet to keep going. The drawbridge part of the
span bounced and shook as the cube trucks and tractor-
trailers rumbled from borough to borough. He hurried to
the Queens side, where the concrete walkway resumed with
its comforting chain-link barrier. Jack ran, looking up from
his feet just long enough to spot Chloe. He took in as little
of the big grey sky, the Manhattan skyline, the tank farms,
the railroad yards, and the tolls for the Midtown Tunnel as
he could. At the bottom of the hill, Chloe followed the sidewalk around and made a left on Jackson Avenue. She disappeared for a moment. When Jack made the turn he saw her
white hair bouncing down into the subway.

Standing on the platform felt good to Jack. He liked the
white tile, the sturdy arched supports, the close atmosphere.
He liked being under the protective cover of the ground.
Having learned, on his first subway ride, to stand clear of

the closing doors, Jack was mostly concerned with avoiding eye contact.

It was easy to distinguish Chloe in the crowd of people waiting for the 7. The only person with a long black tube and a shock of white hair, she was reading *Neuromancer* and impatiently tapping her foot. To hide his face while he watched her, Jack bought a paper from the homeless guy who had stolen a selection from the machines on the corner. Faced with the choice of the *Journal,* the *Times,* the *News,* and the *Post*, Jack picked the *Post*, because that's what he saw the guy in front of him do. He leaned against the dirty tile and idly flipped pages from back to front, catching up on the hubris of the Yankees, the outrageous fare increases proposed by the MTA, the horrors of the lunches served in the middle schools in the Bronx, Liza Minelli, Leona Hemsley, Ivana Trump, Michael Jackson, and a cop who took a bullet for a rapper who was mistaken for a mugger by a deranged vigilante in Flatbush. Jack was pleased with his spycraft, peering over the pages, ostensibly looking for the train, but always keeping Chloe in sight.

A tumble of stale air rolled through the station, announcing the imminent arrival of the 7 train. Commuters stirred, nudging shoulders, crowding the orange safety stripe and hugging the steel columns at the platform's edge. Everyone looked forward and left, toward the oncoming train. Jack stayed in front of Chloe and in her blind spot. When the train arrived, Jack made sure to enter the same car as Chloe, forward by one set of doors.

Bing—Bong.

Jack felt extremely conspicuous in the crowded car. He

was sure that Chloe would recognize him if she actually saw him, and he was buzzing with the feeling of a greater sense of exposure—wasn't it obvious that he wasn't from here, not from Queens, not from the City, not from the Topworld? Wouldn't people take one look at him and scream:

"Atlantean spy!"

"Over there, look!"

"Grab him!"

"Question him!"

"Torture him!"

"Find out where he's from!"

"Find out why he's here!"

But they didn't. Nobody really looked at him. Nobody seemed to care that he was there, with them, hurtling through a tunnel under the East River, aimed through the heart of Midtown, through the very center of the world. Jack noticed that the Benetton ads above the windows had nothing on the variety of skin colors and eye shapes of the people riding the train. Maybe that was why nobody pointed at him and screamed. Or maybe it was the camouflage of the *Post*. Watching an attorney with a bullcase of files clutched between his ankles snap and fan the *Times* with elaborate legerdemain to keep one column readable as he followed a story from page to page and section to section, Jack was glad he had gone for the tabloid. Clearly, it took years of practice and a graduate degree to handle the *Times* on the subway.

The first stop was Grand Central, and a lot of the people in the car got off there. Chloe didn't. Now that seats were available, she took one, and Jack moved to the doorway beside her so that he wasn't standing in her line of sight. As the train moved west through Manhattan, Jack developed a new and alarming hypothesis about the commuters around him. Maybe they were only *posing* as the multi-culti citizens of the City, but were *really* the agents of *other* clandestine civilizations—aliens, holograms, robots, dinosaurs, Bigfoots, Loch Ness Monsters? Was anyone who he appeared to be? Were there any regular people on the train at all, or was everyone up to something? Jack finally decided that, in a way, if they were, it would make his job easier. Since he was too busy to call out a spy from Phobos, it followed that the spy from Phobos would be too busy to blow the whistle on him.

The last stop was Times Square. The doors opened and people poured out of the train. Jack followed Chloe up stairways, through tunnels, up more stairs and out into the street, into the dizzy, dizzy lights and crowds and cops and cars and discount theater tickets and "Come to the comedy club" and "Have you met your Savior, Jesus Christ?" It was too much to take in, there was too much to see to really see it, so Jack ignored everything except the white-haired girl in black who, as she stomped uptown along Broadway, never broke her determined stride.

The black glass-and-steel tower was set back from the street on its own marble plateau, a semi-public platform scattered with benches, shrubs and trees, smokers, jugglers and homeless people. It had four constantly revolving revolving doors that churned through the building's workers, hurling them out from the lobby and sucking them in from outside when they got too close.

Chloe was drawn up the steps and pulled inside. Jack followed at what he hoped was the optimum following distance. She had obviously been in the lobby before—she didn't pay attention to the piano player or the waterfall or the newsstand or the "kaffebar." She didn't bother with the information/security desk or the electronic directory kiosk. She walked by the elevator bank for floors 1-15 and joined the people waiting for the cars that would take them to 16-30.

Jack hung back. He had to ride in the same car with Chloe, unnoticed. A bell chimed and the glass circle above the doors closest to Jack lit up. The elevator had arrived. Jack pretended to hold a cell phone to his ear and began shouting. "Tuesday? I told you Monday! This is no good. No good! The numbers are terrible, what? You're breaking up! Of course I'm on a cell phone! What? I told you Monday! Tuesday? Monday!" Obliviously, he stomped past the people who had been waiting patiently for the elevator. He timed it perfectly. Just as the doors opened, he kept his head down and pushed his way inside and to the back corner through the people getting off. As he hoped they would, the people who got on behind him immediately turned to face the doors. He gave his fake conversation a final "What? I can't hear you! I'll call you from my desk," and then swayed at the knees as the doors shut and the thing shot up fifteen stories in four seconds. With a sickening change in velocity, it stopped at sixteen. The doors opened, a couple of businessmen got out, the doors closed and opened again at nineteen. Chloe remained, leaning against the side of the car, nodding to the music in her headphones.

At twenty-six, Chloe tightened her grip on her portfolio and slipped her headphones off her ears, dropping them around her neck. At twenty-eight, the doors opened and she got off and Jack had to hold onto the horizontal bar that ran waist-high around the elevator to keep from falling over. Through the floor-to-ceiling windows beyond a lot of white furniture, Jack saw what it meant to be twenty-eight floors up in the sky. He had never been at such an altitude, and it deeply freaked him out. As the doors were closing, Jack summoned the presence of mind to take note of the name of the company etched into the glass—TRITON ARCHITECTURE. When the doors had shut and Jack could stand successfully again, the suit who remained with him said, "What do you do? Internet?" He pointed at Jack's flip-flops.

"Yeah. Internet."

The suit stepped closer and looked into Jack's face. "I'm not a doctor," he said, "but I think you should get your eye looked at. You've got something growing in there," and then the bell chimed, the doors opened, and he got off on twenty-nine.

Jack slumped against the back wall and wiped some yellow goo from his itchy eyes. The Newtown Creek had gotten him good.

As Jack was swept up in the revolving door and expelled from the building, two men wearing black suits and gold ties fell in on either side of him. Each grasped one of Jack's arms just above the elbow, and steered him to the sidewalk and around the corner. A black Lincoln Navigator sat at a hydrant with its engine running, dropping 808 booms so deep from its formidable subs they were felt in the gut rather than heard. The windows were tinted illicitly dark, and the front door was labeled in gold stick-on letters—*Malta Knights Mediterranean Imports LIC NY*—and a small decal of a red flag with a white diagonal stripe and a gold cross.

One of the Goldties opened the rear door and got in, sliding across the leather seat to the far side. Jack stomped on the toe of the other one and tried to run, but he grabbed Jack and pushed him into the oversized SUV, then got in and shut the door. The Goldties took Jack's backpack from him and rifled through his pockets. The driver, whose hair and gold tracksuit smelled damp, pulled into traffic. In the mirror, Jack could see that his eyes were bloodshot and weepy. From the passenger seat, a small dog barked, high and sharp. The person holding it murmured soothingly in Latin and turned down the west-coast hip-hop on the system. A gold plastic crown on the dashboard reeked of artificial vanilla.

Jack craned his neck around, trying to see what was in the cavernous cargo area behind him. He spotted cases of anchovies and sardines labeled with the Maltese diver-flag logo and a folding handtruck before a rough hand grabbed his chin and yanked his head forward again. A very old face of indeterminate gender peered at him over the center console upon which sat a tiny growling dog with silken white hair. A three-pronged metal claw clutched one of Jack's business cards. The old face laughed malevolently, the wide-set eyes sparkled.

"I am called Gozo. And you are . . ." croaked the ancient creature as he (or she) glanced at Jack's card, ". . . Jack Fish. Ha! An excellent name for what you really are. Would you not agree, son of Atlas?"

"I don't know what you mean," Jack lied.

"Very well. You don't know what I mean. *Hem.*"

"How is the sardine business?" Jack countered with a sneer.

Gozo answered, "Tell me, Jack Fish—would you recommend the Polaris 360?"

Jack unwittingly took the bait. "What's a Polaris 360?"

"It's a scum-eating pool robot."

When the mocking laughter from the henchmen died down, Gozo asked with false naiveté, "You are a pool supply supplier, are you not?"

"Why? Do you have a pool?" Jack snapped.

Pleased to have irked him, Gozo said, "No, I do not."

"When you get one, call me. *I'll* take care of you personally." Jack knew he should stop with the tough-guy comebacks, but he couldn't help it.

The Goldtie put Jack's stuff back in his backpack, except for the Swiss Army Knife, which he pocketed.

Ancient Gozo took a rubber frankfurter out of the glove compartment and gave it to the dog, who pounced on it, snarling and drooling. Then he (or she) turned back to Jack and said, "Why do you hate me, Jack? We are not so different, you and I. Oh no. Not so different as you think at all. *Hem.*"

Jack managed to say nothing.

Gozo continued, "Jack, do you know why your masters fear and loathe my people so much? Do you know what lies at the center of our feud? Our rivalry?"

"Doesn't matter," Jack spat. "We're not rivals. We're enemies. That's all I need to know."

"No, Jack. You need to know *why*. And there's another *why* you need to know as well. The why of why your masters won't tell you *why*. Why is that, don't you wish to know?"

"No. I don't need to know why. And don't ask me why I don't need to know. I don't care." Jack said, unconvincingly, even to himself. *Why* are *the Maltese our enemies?* he wondered for the first time. *If nobody up here knows that we exist, how can we have enemies on the Topworld?*

Gozo leaned around the seat and looked Jack in the eye. "The philosophers have said that there is no hatred stronger than that between brothers, Jack. Don't you see? We are of the same stock. Remnants. Survivors. Titans. The last of the greatest civilization the world has ever known. We are the same, only you are wet and I," Gozo inserted a cackle, "am dry!"

"Whaleshit. You don't know what you're talking about."

"Don't I? Jack, I think you'll find that I know quite a bit about what I'm talking about. While your masters quiver, hidden in the muck, burning blubber for light and heat when they have access to unlimited raw power, there are others of us—yes, us, Jack, we, us—who live in the sunlight and the air and are ready to act, ready to make ourselves and the hidden power known."

The Navigator was in the West Village now. It pulled up to the hydrant in front of a ravioli shop, and the driver got out of the truck, went around back, and opened the tailgate. Jack swiveled, looking for an opening to escape. The driver gave him a hateful look through squinty, gooey eyes as he grabbed two cases of anchovies. The Goldties held Jack's arms in the lobsterlike grip of their calloused hands while they nodded their heads to Snoop rapping lugubriously about his enormous testicles.

The driver returned and handed a square white box to Gozo.

"*Gratias agere.* Well done," he (or she) said. He (or she) then opened the box, took out a cannoli, and placed it on the console for the dog, who eagerly began to lick the almondy filling from the pastry tube. Then he (or she) took one for him (or herself) and passed the box back to the Goldtie, who offered it to Jack.

"Thank you," he said, and took one. It was sweet, but not too sweet, the rich filling was light and creamy, and the pastry had a satisfying chew to it—delicious. The Goldties took their cannoli and the box was passed to the driver who nabbed the last one. Nobody spoke as they nibbled and munched on their afternoon snack. Gozo's empty gums made soft wet sounds as he (or she) crushed the pastry against the roof of his (or her) mouth with his (or her) wormy tongue.

The Navigator navigated West Street south and wrapped around the tip of Manhattan, then picked up the FDR by the South Street Seaport. Gozo sat idly stroking the dog with his (or her) claw in contemplative silence, then suddenly croaked, "It is too much for you, Jack Fish. It goes against all that you have learned, all that you have known to be so in your short life. I will stop lecturing you. You don't need to have a greater understanding quite yet. You need only apprehend one thing."

Large hands took Jack by the shoulders and pushed him forward over the center console. The dog licked cannoli off his chin. Gozo leaned into Jack's face and hissed, "You are looking for someone. You think that you are very close to finding him."

"I'm a pool supply salesman," Jack lamely asserted.

"Do not get any closer. Instead, go back. Go back and tell your masters that he whom you seek cannot be found. Do this today."

"Why should I?" demanded Jack, abandoning his thin cover in annoyance.

"Because otherwise we will kill you. Either of the men sitting beside you would be happy to do it. Our driver has already asked me permission several times. Do you understand?"

"What I don't understand is why you don't just kill me now."

Gozo smiled a horrible, toothless smile and said, "How will you deliver my message if you are dead?"

Jack was yanked back against the seat where he pouted in impotent rage. The obese truck straddled the lanes on the crooked, rolling highway cantilevered onto the edge of the island. It lurched and drifted, lunged and bounced, and Jack felt sick, not landsick or drug sick, but carsick from the gummy suspension overcompensating for the ragged road. After they passed the austere slab of the UN, where Atlantis had no official representation, the city built itself over the highway, and they entered a three-sided tunnel under huge hospital buildings, with one wall open to the furious river only a few feet below. The driver exited and brought them up and around onto the 59th Street Bridge.

Gozo's shriveled face appeared again over the console. "Your mission has ended, Jack Fish. You will not find your rogue. It is your decision whether you return to your masters empty-handed or missing your head. Do what I tell you, and when an old star shines again, you will be remembered as one who helped us. There are those of us, yes, us, Jack, who are ready to reclaim the ten thrones and rule the world as we once did. And that time is very soon. Very soon, indeed. *Hem.*"

As the Navigator rolled off the bridge into the mess of Queens Plaza, the man on Jack's left removed a chemically soaked handkerchief from a baggie and held it to Jack's face as the man on his right took the saliva-covered lead-filled frankfurter from the dog and raised it, ready to strike Jack in the back of the head.

The ancient voice croaked, "Now, you will sleep with the fishes. *Hem.*"

J ack came to, sputtering in the putrid darkness of a Dumpster half full of decomposing anchovies and sardines. It was like being inside the belly of a whale, something Jack remembered well from junior high. The available air in the box was hot and thick with pungent rot, barely breathable even to someone good at breathing, which Jack still was not. He tried to sit up but hit his head on the lid, ringing the bin like a muffled gong. Falling back down, Jack put his feet on the lid and shoved, flipping it open and pushing himself a little deeper into the foul slurry of scales, heads, tails, bones, guts, tomato sauce, and oil. He managed to tumble out and collapse in the gutter. It was night, and Jack didn't know if he'd been in the Dumpster for hours or days.

Jack stumbled along deserted sidewalks through a canyon

of shut steel roller gates illegibly scrawled with the tags that proclaimed identity to an indifferent city. It was a conversation by, for, and about its own culture that took place on everyone else's walls, an unrecognizable call for recognition. Jack turned a corner and walked a few blocks under elevated tracks that shook with a passing N train. A single skyscraper jutted up from the foreground, a displaced teal glass tower jarringly incongruous in this four-story world, a Gulliver among the Lilliputians, looking forlornly at its tall friends across the river in Manhattan. Jack aimed for it, lacking any other distinguishing landmarks he might use for navigation. He hit a block where a few things were open, a diner, a newsstand, and a pool supply showroom and warehouse— an A.T. Landis Pool Supply Showroom and Warehouse. *So we actually do sell pool supplies!*

Soggy, smelly, and ebullient, Jack went inside. Rows of hot tubs and inflatable palm trees and pails of chlorine dotted the floor. A layer of dust covered everything. A silver-haired woman wearing an eye-patch stood behind the counter. She looked up at Jack and said, suspiciously, "Can we help you?"

Giddy with his luck in finding the place, Jack blurted, "Yeah, uh, hey—do you sell the Polaris 360?"

The lady's one visible eye grew wide as her hands disappeared under the counter.

Jack offered, "It's a scum-eating—"

"Hands in the air, mouthbreeder!" She had a sprung-and-loaded speargun with the pointy blue tip of a twin spinner rockpoint mere inches from Jack's forehead. Her good eye stared at him down the shaft. "This thing has enough punch to go right through a Mako at five meters, so don't try anything stupid. Barnacles! I should have smelled your anchovy breath the second you walked in here. Now, get on your knees!"

Jack gasped, tried to protest, but the words wouldn't come, so he dutifully dropped to his knees.

"Bob!" she called out, never taking her eye off Jack. "Bob, come up front please, and see what the tide washed in!"

A balding man with huge eyebrows and wide-set eyes appeared next to the woman. He wiped his hands on his pants and said through a mouthful of half-chewed food, "'nother Maltese stooge? Well, he won't get past my Flo, will he? Ha!"

"I'm not a—"

"Face down on the floor, then, Savior of Europe."

"I'm an Agent—The Left Prong! We're on the same side."

"Of course you'd say that, you sardine salesman. Hands behind your back."

Jack did as he was told. Strong hands grabbed his wrists and bound them with nylon cord, then lifted him to his feet.

"Let's go with you, then. Into the back room. We can't have our customers see you like this. By Oceanus, you stink."

The back room was set up as a small apartment, tidy as a ship's cabin, with a kitchenette, a bed, a couch, chair, and a row of security camera monitors. A plastic Poseidon statue with a clock in its base stood on a stumpy ceramic column. On a chest against the wall, a black-and-white television was showing water polo on ESPN2. Jack didn't struggle when Bob took his wallet out of his pocket. He already had Jack's back-pack, and dumping the contents out on a table, he grunted in derision. Then he pushed Jack firmly toward the leather recliner, which had been patched in places with duct tape. Jack sat down heavily. He felt like he was back in his dad's den.

Jack tried again. "Look, I guess I said the wrong thing when I came in here, but I'm Agent Jack Fish, I'm up on a mission, and I've just been threatened and dumped by the Maltese. Check my tattoo. I can prove it!"

Flo sat down on a wooden stool with the spear gun in her lap. "All right," she said. "Prove it. Did Atlantis build the pyramids?"

"Mayan or Egyptian?"

She arched a brow. "Hmm. What is Atlantis's greatest gift to civilization on both sides of the Atlantic?"

"The banana! No seeds! Lots of potassium! Comes in its own wrapper!"

"OK, then. True or false, Atlantis was founded by aliens."

"False!"

"Atlantis invented the laser."

"True."

"The gas grill."

"False."

"The ottoman."

"True!"

"The condominium."

"True!"

"Baa! This proves nothing." Her face clouded over in dark thought, then brightened. "I know." She sang, "They taste so sweet . . ."

Jack automatically supplied the next line of the jingle he'd heard since childhood, "They cook up quick!"

Bob sang the harmony with Flo, "They can't be beat!"

Jack came back in with, "The Titan's pick!"

They sang the rest ensemble-style, "For cen-tur-ies the tasty treat! Deep-C Fish Sticks! Deep-C Fish Sticks!"

Bob held up Jack's I ♥ FISHING keychain. "Well, he's got it."

Flo looked hard at Jack for a moment, and broke into a warm smile. "I think you're one of ours, after all."

Bob said, "Stand up then, Jack Fish. Let's get your hands untied. Sorry we're so suspicious, but we've had a couple of attempts at infiltrating our filtration business, if you see what I mean. Ha!"

"Bob, give him some of your things to wear." Flo engaged the safety on her spear gun and stood it against the wall.

Bob gave Jack his backpack and wallet back. Then he tossed him a clean I ♥ NY T-Shirt, a sweatshirt that read THE CHLORINATOR and a pair of stiff dark blue Wrangler jeans. Jack went into the little bathroom to change.

When he reentered the room, Flo was pouring the last of three cans of Clamato into glasses. She gave one to each of the men, and opened a bag of pizza-flavored Goldfish crackers. Bob sat on the couch where he could see both the TV and Jack without turning his head and resumed eating his tuna sandwich. Jack sat back down in the lounge chair and took a sip of his clam-and-tomato juice.

He said, "I can't believe they didn't tell me this place was here."

Bob looked at Flo, then at Jack. He asked, surprised, "What about your business cards?"

"What, this?" said Jack, fishing out a soggy, smelly, limp Jack Fish, Pool Supply Salesman card.

"Did you ever turn it over, read the back?" Bob asked as if speaking to a small child.

Jack shook his head in the negative and flipped the card over. Printed on the back were five locations in the tri-state area, including the 24-hour Queens outpost.

"Oh," he said, feeling dumb. "Why are you open twenty-four hours, anyway?"

Bob laughed. "So when the Maltese dump you four blocks away, you have someplace to go. You're not the first one of our guys to get thrown out with the trash and stagger in here after midnight."

"But do you ever actually sell pool supplies in the middle of the night?"

"Oh, sure. Just last week, some rapper guy came in at three in the morning, needed a replacement motor for his Jacuzzi right away. He had a pair of panties stuck in there somewhere, the thing burned out—"

Flo interrupted, "But that's just for cover, of course. We're here for when the Agents need us, and to keep an eye on the twenty-four-hour Anchovy Distributor where you woke up."

"It doesn't seem all that exciting."

Flo pointed to her eyepatch. "This is what comes from excitement, young Jack Fish. Someone has to keep the light on for you. And at this point in my life, I'd just as well be on this side of the counter, instead of waking up in Dumpsters."

She added conversationally, "Now, what are you up here doing, dear?"

"I'm looking for Victor Sargasso. He was an agent, disappeared." Jack decided not to tell the old couple he'd almost found him.

Bob slammed his palm down on the arm of the couch. "Giant Clam!" he roared.

Jack gave him a confused look.

"Sargasso. Why are they so worried about him? Agents disappear all the time, but they can't let go of Victor Sargasso. Big waste, if you ask me, 'specially when there are more important things missing than Victor Sargasso."

"Oh, stop it Bob. We'll be back home soon enough, and then you'll be complaining about the food again." Flo reminded him.

Bob took a long drink and let out a long sigh. Then he said, "One of the Stars goes missing, I think that's the top priority that's all, if you believe them things caused the deluge in the first place. Course, I don't."

"A Star is missing? That's alarming," said Jack, a little alarmed.

"Well, maybe yes, maybe no. Elders only check on them every decade or so. When they opened the vaults last year, there's only two Stars in bed. Now, that's a concern, I'll warrant, but why does it mean that there will be no rotation of Pool Supply personnel until the damn thing is located? It could have been missing for eighteen years already!" Bob paused to drink noisily, then picked up where he left off. "Nobody has seen it up here or down below, and nobody knows how to use it anyway. And they have you running around looking for Victor Sargasso, and me staying up all night waiting for you to show up at the front door reeking of anchovy guts. How'd you plan on doing Sargasso anyway? With your odor!"

Bob got up from the couch laughing to himself and took a wooden case out of a drawer. He opened the case and said, "Here. You'd better take this," and handed Jack a well-used speargun, a foot-and-a-half long, the wooden grip and steel barrel rubbed to a warm patina. "My old mini cave gun. I won't be getting into too many more melees. It's all set up for air combat. Got a nickel tip on that sharpie!"

Jack put it in his backpack and solemnly thanked him.

"I'll call you a car. You should get back to your safe-house."

Jack finished his Clamato and got up to wait by the front of the store. Bob stood with him.

"Ever have steak? I'll take you to Peter Luger's sometime. It's the one good thing about being up here."

A black Town Car pulled up.

"Well, try to stay out of the Dumpsters anyway," Bob said, closing the car door. He gave Jack the three-finger Trident salute, knocked twice on the roof, and the car zoomed away.

J ack had seen enough of the architect dress code to select flat-front black trousers and a tight-knit charcoal gray cotton mock-turtleneck sweater from the wardrobe in the safehouse closet. He found a tin of Hairgum pomade in the medicine cabinet and smushed his hair around until it attained a calculated nonchalance. Thin orange-and-yellow striped socks provided a bit of contained rebellious contrast to the black Kenneth Coles with elastic heel cups that felt so good on his feet. He shouldered his backpack and felt the weight of the mini-gun on his spine. At 8:15 he walked out the safehouse door. Jack grabbed the *Post* and a cup of coffee at the Deli Mart and trotted down the stairs of the subway to join the morning rush waiting for the L train. He looked like a young architect on his way to work at the big midtown firm, because he kind of was.

Jack tried to read up on the Mayor's war with ferrets and the off-season mismanagement of the Jets, but he couldn't concentrate on the words through the persistent images of the terrible things he had seen from the twenty-eighth floor. He tried to prepare himself for what he had to do, to convince himself that it was perfectly normal to work hundreds of feet up in the sky, but fundamentally, he couldn't believe it. The very premise of an office tower was unnatural and absurd—desks and bathrooms and fax machines and acres of commercial carpet all kept from plummeting through space and gravity by less than an inch of plate glass. *These people are crazy.* They puttered around with their files and reports, obsessing about the politics of their petty office worlds when the real problem was that they were standing on rickety pillars of concrete and metal with nothing around them but the very thin air.

A group of office workers trudged across the obsidian plateau toward the grasping paddles of the revolving doors. Jack was carried along with them, drawn into the building, involuntarily pulled toward the banks of elevators. Security nodded generically at the dozens of busy people starting their busy days. As long as you weren't wearing a messenger bag or carrying an unconcealed weapon, you were free to walk right in and visit any floor you liked.

As the crowded elevator car approached the twenty-eighth floor, Jack reached into his backpack and, careful not to reveal the mini-gun, withdrew a pair of reading glasses he'd picked up at a Duane Reed, along with a pack of

Original Flavor Trident and a bottle of eyedrops. He put on the glasses as the doors opened and stepped out into the blurry white reception area of Triton Architecture. He had made it in before nine, and the desk was unmanned. A group of the untitled workers that kept the firm going got off the elevator with Jack. Someone held the door for him, and he was in.

Jack was pleased with his spycraft—the glasses blurred everything directly in front of him, effectively eliminating the terrifying view out the windows. Peering alternately above and below the thick lenses, Jack managed not to bump into anything as he moved toward the sheltered core of the building. For balance, he ran his hand along rows of white file cabinets that defined the corridor and separated it from the pods and workstations of the various studios: Corporate, Education and Institution; Fixtures, Furniture and Equipment; Residential; Government; Entertainment and Exhibition. Clusters of workers, coffees and bagels and smoothies in hand, eyeballed Jack as he walked past their neat, uncluttered desks, taking his measure, not as an imposter, but as a potential competitor.

Jack tried to avoid meeting anyone's eyes. Instead, he looked at the examples of the work the firm produced that were on display around the office. Presentation drawings were mounted on foamcore and tacked to the walls. Chipboard models formed a miniature unplanned city atop the cabinets. Office buildings rubbed shoulders with churches and honeycombed villages of the future. The yo-yo shaped headquarters of a midwestern yo-yo manufacturer was jammed in between a Finnish curling stadium and a waterslide that emerged from the mouth of a Sphinx. Jack leaned in for a closer look but was brought around by an insistant thump on his shoulder.

"Are you my intern?" barked a pasty young man dressed all in black, with narrow-framed fashion eyewear and a ripe pimple on his forehead.

"Me?" Jack quickly decided that he was. "Yes, sir! I am your intern."

"Where the hell have you been? We have a presentation for the project manager in twenty minutes. I need solid surface samples. Pull me all the good Corian whites. Not the fake stone ones, and *not* the ones with the stupid confetti in them. The *good* whites. Also, I need the autoflush urinal valve in brushed chrome, and a venti chai latte. I'll be in the conference room setting up."

He ripped a Pepto-pink Post-It off a pad and stuck it on Jack's hand. Jack stared at it dumbly.

"In the materials library. Conrad will help you. Go!" He grabbed Jack by the shoulders and spun him around, then gave a little push to the lower back that sent Jack forward down the hall.

When he was safely within the confines of the metal shelves lined with fat binders and catalogs and masonite display boards, Jack took off his glasses and poked around. On one shelf, plastic bins were loaded with slices of rock in colors from the deepest indigo to the starkest white. On another, he saw more kinds of tile than he knew existed. The next aisle was devoted to metal—hard squares of various alloys brushed, distressed, clear-coated, and raw. There were racks of flooring samples from recycled barn wood to bamboo, the full spectrum of laminates in chips that hung on little hooks on a rotating kiosk, miniature windows, blinds, doors, doorknobs, doorknockers, peepholes—Jack was about to give up on finding whatever it was that his new boss wanted when a silky voice behind him said, "What do you need, honey?"

It was Conrad, the effeminate and super-territorial materials librarian, and this was his library.

Jack showed Conrad his pink list and said, as helplessly as he could, "Corian? Not the stoney kind. And a brushed-chrome automatic-flushing urinal thingy. And where can I get a chai latte around here?"

Conrad nodded. "Did Gordon yell at you? *Bitch*. Don't mind him. His thong is probably riding high again. And don't tell him I told you or they'll have me explaining to HR why I'm still saying 'thong' in the office after I was warned about using the words 'rubber' and 'nipple' when not talking specifically about flooring or plumbing."

Conrad hummed to himself as he grabbed an empty wooden tray off a stack and scurried around his domain, pulling product specs from binders and samples from drawers and bins. He handed Jack the loaded tray. "Here's your Corian and your self-flusher. The latte is in the lobby. And if you bring me back one of those fat-free banana muffins, I'll give you a few pointers on how this place works."

"Banana muffin? Sure. Just let me give this stuff to Gordon."

"Make three lefts when you walk out of here."

Fortunately for Jack, the conference rooms were grouped together in the windowless interior reaches of the floor. He found Gordon standing on a chair, pinning sketches on yellow trace to the gray fabric wall. Gordon nodded at the glass table, and Jack put the tray down, and escaped.

Twenty minutes later, Jack and Conrad were sitting at a small white Saarinen side table behind racks of cedar shingles and a stack of glass block.

"So. What can you tell me about Triton?" Jack asked.

Conrad brushed low-fat crumbs from his lip and said, "It's just like any other bloated, bureaucratic, hierarchical company. Too many chiefs and not enough Indians, right? Well, lots of Indians and Pakistanis, but that's not what I mean. Lots of fear. Take Gordon, for instance. Gordon is stressed out because he came here to design the City of Tomorrow, and they've had him doing bathrooms for two years, wasting his talents on details for Education and Institution. But he's so afraid of getting let go that he'll never ask for a transfer, and that's exactly why he won't get promoted."

"Aha," Jack said knowingly. He let Conrad ramble on, hoping for some accidental information on Victor Sargasso.

"You don't have to listen to Gordon," Conrad was saying, "The person you *do* have to listen to is Roger, who is the Project Manager of your group and controls all the money and therefore your time. The other person you need to listen to is Lisette, because she's the designer on Gordon's team, and as corporate as this place is, or maybe *because* of how corporate this place is, everyone is completely terrified of the designers."

"Why are they terrified of the designers?"

Conrad rolled his eyes. "The designers are sooo eccentric

and brilliant, they get all inspired and come running into meetings late and say, 'polished concrete' or 'absinthe green' or whatever bullshit they've come up with, and everyone else has to actually do the drawings and endless details and stay late to fix the plotters."

"Right," agreed Jack, not knowing or caring what a plotter was or why it would need fixing at any time of day.

Conrad leaned in and put his hand on Jack's shoulder. "You seem like a smart guy, creative, idealistic, full of big dreams. Look, this may sound crazy, but whatever you do, don't let them promote you."

"Really? Why?"

"Because when they promote you, you start to owe the company more and more, you become fat and lazy, you can't get off the company pipe, and you become too frightened to go anyplace else. And then they have you!"

"What about you?" asked Jack with a smile. "Do they have you?"

"Me? Oh no, not me. I'm just the librarian. All the drama happens around me. This is my domain, my island. As long as I have my samples organized, nobody bothers me." Conrad glanced at an M&Co. clock with the numbers out of order and stood up. "You'd better go find your desk. That meeting must be over by now."

"Can I take something with me?" Jack asked. "I'd like to learn everything I can while I'm here."

"Whatever you want." Conrad made a wide gesture with his hands. "Just sign it out."

Jack grabbed a binder at random—specs for TOTO high-performance toilets with Washlet™ hygienic seats.

He thanked Conrad for the chat and walked purposefully out of the library in no particular direction. Jack was cruising the row of pickled beech doors looking for Sargasso's nameplate when he felt a tap on his shoulder.

When he turned, Gordon thrust a tray into his gut. Jack looked into it and saw arcane curves, lead holders, a compass, and a scale, then looked up at Gordon's scowling face.

"Here are your tools," he snapped. "There's a lot of work to do. Follow me."

Gordon led Jack through the open-plan maze of steel desks and white cabinets and partitions. Busy, serious, diligent men and women in their thirties, wearing expensively uncomplicated clothing, worked in quiet tension at oversized monitors. Anyone who had to talk did so at a controlled and contained volume, and for as short a time as possible. There was no music or laughter, only the plastic crunching of computer keyboards and the raspy strokes of lead on paper. It was clear that whatever everyone was doing, it was extremely important.

Gordon stopped by an empty desk in a cluster of five and pointed to a black ergonomical task chair with a five-star base. He said, "That's your seat. For the rest of the day I want you to get familiar with the software we use. Pick up these redlines, and tell me when you're done." He threw a stack of drawings onto Jack's new desk.

"No problem," Jack said with forced confidence. "I'll pick up the redlines, and I'll tell you when I'm done."

Gordon grunted and hurried off to find the Senior Associate and tell her that the PM had approved the fixtures for the German men's room.

Jack laid the drawings out with care, and managed to bring up something complicated-looking on the computer screen. Satisfied that he had created the convincing impression that he was working as hard as anyone else, he opened the single drawer under his desktop. Inside he found a wad of napkins, packets of soy and duck sauces, a Piyu-Piyu pencil sharpener with a grinning yellow duck printed on the side, and the company phone directory from the previous year. He thumbed through it and felt a victorious surge when he saw the entry: VICTOR SARGASSO, DESIGNER. So Johnny Belmont *had* been helpful, in his self-interested way. Chloe had lead him to Sargasso, and now he could complete his mission and kill him.

Jack stood up. Then he sat back down. *Wait, Jack, wait.* He would wait. What was he going to do? Call Sargasso to a meeting and shoot him when he arrived? No. Jack knew he should be methodical. Study the layout. Learn about Sargasso's habits. Create an opportunity. Develop an escape plan. And find out what was going on—why *did* Chloe bring a drawing of the Palace of Poseidon here?

The phonebook said that Sargasso was in the E&E studio—Entertainment and Exhibition—who did big stuff like stadiums and concert halls. And he was the studio designer, which gave him a lot of clout, from what Conrad had said.

Jack's flat front pants were tight around the thighs. He emptied his pockets to reduce the strain, and he had to look twice at the pack of gum before it registered—Original Flavor Trident. Citizens of the Topworld assumed that meant some kind of blue mint, but the Original Flavor originated in Atlantis, as did the whole idea of chewing gum. He carefully opened the pack and spread the wrapper out flat on his desk, back side up. Trident was having a sweepstakes, and there was a lot of fine print in a light ink that told the gum chewer just how unlikely it was that they would win the personal submarine, the trip to Cuba, or the scuba lessons. Jack knew that, in fact, it was impossible to win any of the prizes, as the fine print describing the sweepstakes and its prizes was actually code intended for Agents like him. Instead of picking up redlines, Jack spent the next three-quarters of an hour decrypting the monthly bulletin to all Agents. When he had eliminated the irrelevant words like *no purchase necessary*, and *void where prohibited*, Jack came up with the message. MALT EASE SEEK MAP. He nodded. He knew that. Lesson two at spy school was that the Maltese were obsessed with the layout and location of the Royal Metropolis. But it was the second part of the message that Jack found disturbing, the part that said, ENTER TODAY AND DON'T LET THE STAR FISH GET AWAY!

Gordon's sweaty, spotty face loomed over the low partition.

"She signed off, so it's a go. Now the fun begins. I need you to get me a turkey-and-roasted-red-pepper pannini and a Diet Coke. Are you almost done with those redlines?"

"Almost!" Jack falsely assured him, getting to his feet.

Jack was careful to appear busy for the rest of the day despite his inability to do any actual work. He stuck his head into file cabinets, unrolled and re-rolled drawings, and hurried around the office, trying to locate Victor Sargasso while avoiding looking out the windows. When a decent interval had transpired, Jack returned his toilet seat binder to the materials library and casually struck up another conversation with Conrad.

"You know," Jack said. "They've completely eliminated the need for toilet paper with these things?"

"Oh yeah. There are millions of 'em in Japan. Fantastic. Cleanest asses in the world."

Jack couldn't think of a way to segue from that so he simply said, "I think I'd really like to work with the E&E people. They seem to have the most interesting projects."

Conrad gave Jack a jaded look. "*Of course* you do. E&E does the sexiest stuff—*everyone* wants to work for E&E. We don't build cathedrals anymore, do we? We build sports complexes and entertainment arenas. Every city has to have one to prove it's worth anything. Take a number. Get in line, darling."

"And the designer, Victor somebody?"

"Sargasso. Brilliant. Dead charming, though not on my team from what I can find out. But there's a rumor—"

"Rumor?" asked Jack, very interested.

Conrad lowered his voice. "Nobody has seen his license. Or even a diploma. Nothing. Some people, I think they're just jealous of him, but they say that he's not even an architect. He comes in at noon, he leaves at midnight, he breezes in and out of meetings with his scarf trailing behind him like an aviator. He always has something brilliant and new, but they say he's untaught, completely improvising." Conrad smiled with glee at the thought of the hoax. "And everyone is way too intimidated to ask him!"

"I'd really love to transfer to that studio. I mean, Gordon's bathrooms are exquisite, but—"

"You need to talk to Heather. Go out here and walk straight back until you see the tall black girl. Tell her I sent you, and that I said you were the hot-shit new talent and they should grab you before you're stuck in fixtures forever. I can't promise anything, honey, but she's the Project Manager over there and she makes it happen."

Jack thanked Conrad again, and following his directions, found Heather easily enough. More importantly, he found the home of the Entertainment and Exhibition Studio, which was in its own lobe of the floorplan, self-contained and somewhat removed from the rest of the firm. Jack walked through the studio purposefully, without stopping to talk to anyone or drop off anything. Jack knew that if he kept walking at a constant speed and took each turn as if he knew exactly where he was going, he probably wouldn't be noticed. For his part, he tried to notice everything and everyone. Along the outside wall, E&E had three private offices with pickled beech doors, and one was open a crack and marked with a nameplate that read victor sargasso in the pretentious lowercase that was the firm's hallmark. Jack's breath caught and his scrotum tightened, but he did not shout "You scaly bastard! I've got you!" and kick the door down to grab Sargasso's naked throat with his bare hands. No. Once he saw the nameplate, Jack swung his gaze away from the pickled beech door and kept walking, stride unbroken, back through the studio and back to his desk and strident Gordon for the rest of the afternoon. *Right now,* Jack knew, *correcting bathroom details is the job.*

At five, Gordon was pleased to see his new intern diligently working on the pile of drawings that had been assigned him and left to see his dermatologist. At six, most of the office got up and left to go meet people for cocktails. At seven, a couple of people ordered Vietnamese and pushed to make their deadlines. At eight-thirty, Jack picked up his backpack and, skirting any occupied desk, quietly made his way back across the floor to the Entertainment and Exhibition studio.

Heather and the rest had gone, but Jack could see that Sargasso's door was open a crack, and that the light was on inside his office. There was nobody within Jack's line of sight as he slipped his hand into the backpack and his fingers found the trigger of the mini-gun. He pushed the door open. With great relief, Jack saw that the window had been glazed with frosted glass that let in the light, but not the view. The walls, floor, drafting table, and desk were all white and immaculate. At the desk, an extremely handsome man with lustrous black hair looked up from a sketch. He wore a green suit, accented by an orange scarf. He smiled dangerously, sat back, and closed his very green and wide-set eyes.

Now! thought Jack, but he didn't, and as he stood there, immobile, with his hand paralyzed in his backpack, he could feel the moment of opportunity slipping away from him, getting exponentially more distant every nanosecond he waited.

Victor Sargasso opened his eyes and said in a mellifluous voice, "I've been expecting you."

Jack's moment of opportunity was reaching escape velocity. He sputtered, "You have? Me?"

"Of course," Victor Sargasso said mildly. "It was only a matter of time before the Elders would send someone to find me. Maybe you're the first, or the third or the tenth.

What does it matter? You're the one who's here, now. Please, have a seat."

"Thank you," Jack answered and sat down. He immediately regretted it. Lesson six in Assassin class stated that you should always try to be standing up when attempting to kill someone.

"So, now that you have found Victor Sargasso, what will you do with him?" Victor raised an eyebrow, and both men laughed, Jack, a little awkwardly. "Please, I am at a disadvantage. You know my name, but I do not know yours," he paused drolly, "even though it would appear that you might be my employee."

"Oh," said Jack. "I'm Jack. Jack Fish."

"Well met, Jack Fish. What do you think of that chair?"

"Um. Well. . ." Jack shifted his weight around to try it out. "It's very comfortable. Supportive, yet relaxing."

"Well put. It's an Eames—the management chair from their aluminum group. In 1973, Bobby Fisher demanded one before he would sit down to play Gary Kasporov in Reykjavik. When Fisher got one, Kasporov demanded one too."

"Is this a chess match, Mr. Sargasso?"

"Not at all. Please, call me Victor."

"OK, Victor."

"Jack, before you kill me, I'd like to take you to dinner. Someplace we can talk."

"What do we have to talk about? You broke the rules. That's all I need to know. We have the same masters. You know how it works."

"Of course. I'm not denying it, or pleading for my life. Jack, is this your first mission?"

"What difference does that make?"

"I thought it might be. Jack, all I want to do is tell you why I did what I did. Then you can kill me, just like you're supposed to do."

"I don't know," said Jack. His finger rubbed the trigger of the gun. The nickel-plated sharpie tip on the short spear would easily rip through the backpack on its way to Sargasso's chest. All Jack had to do was pull, to move one finger a little bit closer to his palm.

Without breaking eye contact with Jack, Victor rolled up the sketch in front of him, snapped a rubber band around it, and opened a drawer.

"Look at it this way," he said, his eyes and smile steady, his hands busy with activity. "Would *you* want to die on an empty stomach?"

He slipped the sketch away and shut the drawer.

"I suppose not," ventured Jack, his finger slipping a little bit further from his palm.

Victor stood, clapped once, and rubbed his hands together enthusiastically. Jack rose hesitantly.

"I know just what I will have for my final meal. We will go to Yumi's! Jack, you must dine with me. It will be a meal that redefines your experience of what eating can be."

Victor was at the door, his hand on Jack's elbow.

"I don't know," Jack repeated.

Victor's face was very close to Jack's. His eyes sparkled, his breath was sweet as he said softly, "Come. You are to be my executioner, and it is my final wish to dine with you. And as my executioner, you must grant me my final wish. It is our way, need I remind you."

Glad for a chance to psych himself up again to kill Victor, Jack said, "You're right. I cannot deny you your final wish. I will dine with you. Lead the way, Mr. Sargasso."

"Call me Victor," Victor reminded him, as they walked to the elevator, their eyes averted from the terrible view.

They were in a tiny basement restaurant that had no name. Windowless, with a smooth concrete floor and walls, it had the solid, implacable ambience of a prison. There were no tables to sit at, only a pitted steel counter, and upturned 55-gallon drums that served as chairs. The counter stuck through the metal fence, which by dividing the volume of the room in half, defined the space as two cells—one for the customers and one for Yumi, who could not see but was not blind.

"Yumi has not opened her eyes in eight years, and won't open them until her Utopian ideas of the world are realized," said Victor quietly.

"Will that ever happen?" asked Jack.

"Who knows? I'll tell you this, though. She has the freshest fish in the City. Also the sharpest knives and the fastest hands. And rules."

"Rules?"

"Rules. You may only have one piece at a time. But first, you must put five dollars cash in the slot in the middle of the bar."

"If she can't see, don't people just pretend to pay? I mean, you could slip anything into the counter, or palm the bills."

"Nobody would try it. She's telepathic, and she's got her knife."

Yumi held up her eighteen-inch fillet blade.

"What should I—" Jack started, but Victor stopped him with a raised palm.

"You don't order here," he explained in a near-whisper. He pointed to Yumi with his eyebrow as she worked, a blur of steel and fish. "She just knows."

Victor held up two five-dollar bills. Yumi acknowledged them with a slight bow of her head, and Victor slid them into the slot in the bar.

Yumi was so fast that there was only enough delay between ordering and receiving her creations to formulate the faintest mental sketch of an image of the delicacy. To the aficionado, this was enough to begin to salivate in anticipation of the harmonious flavors, textures, and temperatures that started just before the first bite, and echoed long after the piece was gone. What was so remarkable about Yumi's fish was that, unlike the usual letdown, where no matter how sublime the idea of each morsel might be, it was instantly forgotten once the real thing arrived, supplanted with the perfection of the morsel at hand. Yumi never disappointed. She was an Artist, a Master, a Genius.

Small, polished wood blocks slid under the pass-through in the fence.

"Tuna hand rolls!" Victor sighed, his voice resonant with memory, wonder, and pleasure.

Black.

White.

Red.

Green.

Seaweed.

Rice.

Tuna.

Wasabi.

The hand rolls were a string quartet of deceptive simplicity, mathematical tension cloaked in melody and color, four volatile elements bound together in a precise balance of mutual push-pull, a prelude to the meal as a whole, and a summation of Yumi's idealist philosophy in each bite—the sushi served in Plato's cave, the universe redux.

Jack watched Victor, unsure of the ritual he should perform to eat. It turned out to be simple. Victor picked up the trumpet-shaped morsel, looked into its open end, and bit. He closed his eyes, he inhaled deeply through his nostrils, he lifted his eyebrows slightly, and he tilted his head back as he chewed. Jack picked up his hand roll and looked inside. It was wrapped in a square of seaweed thinner and crisper than airmail paper that, once filled, had been twisted into a cone between Yumi's thumb and forefinger, and sealed with a brush of her tongue. Nine perfect cubes of blood red bluefin tuna bedded down in fluffy grains of sweetened, vinegared rice laced with poison green wasabi. Jack took a bite, his eyes rolled back, and the world fell away as he tried to understand what was happening in his mouth.

The nori was utterly dry; it held his teethmarks in an absence in the cone. Having served its structural purpose by delivering its contents, it dissolved in salty wisps like the tears of the naked pre-pubescent children who had dried it in the sun on a black sand beach. The seaweed wrapper gave way to the warm, springy dichotomy of the rice, each grain moist and dry, sweet and tangy, an individual and a part of the matrix that supported the living flesh of the great fish of the sea. Ten years old, a hunter and a soldier, she had been conquered by a hand-thrown harpoon on the Grand Banks mere hours before. Her flesh, only a few degrees cooler than his own, melted across Jack's tongue, joining it in deep protein intimacy. He caught a spray of her last memories, the sudden surge of the chase, the briny draw of water over her gills, the liberation of leaping from wave to wave, and the ultimate agony of the barb in her side. As he started to feel absolved by his empathy, a searing electric green bolt shot to the back of his throat, the base of his nose, the stems of his eyes, and the center of his head. It radiated outward in all directions and was gone. He opened his eyes. The passing of the wasabi had brought him back to the basement. Victor smiled at him weakly, tears squeezing out of the corners of his eyes. The two men didn't speak. They ate, they felt, they knew.

The honest savagery of the world lay just beneath the façade of the thin, dry seaweed skin. The taste of killing was thrilling; one life melted into another, over and over. Each bite was a volume on mortality, on replenishment, on life itself. And death. And the moment, the delicious surrender to the moment in between. If he hadn't already known it, the sushi told him so—Jack wasn't a killer. He could appreciate the boundary of transience and infinity through Yumi's creations, but he couldn't push Victor across it.

Victor smiled and put his chopsticks down. "I envy you," he said. "This is the first time you've really eaten fish, though you've eaten it nearly every meal of your life. I know. I *was* you, not that long ago. The thing is, Jack, that when you're there, you believe that Atlantis is the world the way it should be and that everyone else has it wrong. Well, there is plenty up here that is terribly, terribly wrong, but then there are things like what Yumi creates." He gestured toward Yumi at work at her cutting board.

". . ."

Victor smiled a sad smile. "Jack, it's the same fish. The only difference is in perspective, in appreciation, in technique. But it's still just fish. Right?"

Jack held up two fives, let them fall into the slot, and waited for the next delicacy. Yumi nodded, let a moment pass, and slid two ceramic disks under the fence. Slices of octopus, each bound to a pillow of rice with a band of nori. Octopus; sad in her intelligence, the social aesthete who gathers rocks outside her home simply because she likes them. Yumi's tako was sliced so thinly, the cross sections of tentacle were translucent. In the mouth they resisted the teeth, and sprang back with their last reserves of strength. When they were gone, the taste that remained was of the instant the octopus knew she was at the end of her rock-collecting days.

The adolescent melodrama of sea urchin; the oily despair of mackerel; the wicked sin of salmon skin; the depths of giant clam. Victor and Jack were weeping soundlessly, stuffing Lincolns into the slot in the bar and chewing morsels of Yumi's perfect, tragic creation. She knew when they had experienced enough, and without request or remuneration, she provided them each with a cup of green tea and a dish of flying fish roe, marinated in vinegar, wine, and salt. Rebirth, the spring, the perfect shape of nature, the eggs said *promise*, said *tomorrow*, said *hope* and *love*.

"I think it was the darkness that I hated most," Victor said. "Sitting in the cold wet, burning a chunk of whale for a little bit of light, eating the same krill day after day when I knew there was a whole world above us, a world that *we* created but were too afraid to face . . ."

Jack looked deep into his tea, and the broken bits of leaves augured what he already knew.

"Victor, how am I going to kill you now?"

Yumi discreetly stepped toward the far corner of her work-space, and briskly sharpened her knife.

Victor sipped his tea and said, "Jack, do you know what my last mission was, the one I walked away from? Did they tell you that when they told you to kill me?"

"No."

"I thought not. Jack, I was trained as an assassin, like you. I carried out many missions, and then I was ordered to kill a child, a boy whom the Elders thought was the illegitimate son of one of the Ambassadors. The Elders considered the boy to be a potential leverage point for the Maltese, a vulnerability they wanted to eliminate. I refused. I was recalled. I refused to return.

I was threatened with elimination. So I hid. Not very well, but I hid. I cut off all communication with the Elders, with Landis, with everyone, and I created a new life for myself. And do you know what I found out a year later?"

Jack looked at Victor blankly, then shook his head.

"The boy wasn't the Ambassador's son at all. The Elders had made a mistake, they had bad information. There was no strategic reason for the child to die. I have never regretted doing the right thing, Jack. Never."

Jack took a gulp of his tea, and placed the cup down on the counter. He said, "What am I supposed to do? If I don't kill you, they'll send another agent after me. If he won't kill me, someone else will kill him. There's no end to it, Victor. I have to kill you."

"When you look at it that way, you're right, of course. But Jack, who am I hurting by being alive? I'm a harmless architect. Do I really deserve to die for something I didn't do?"

Jack felt very uncomfortable. Victor's eyes twinkled.

"Well, perhaps you should kill me. But you don't have to do it tonight. I'm not going to run, Jack. I never did, and I won't run now. You know where to find me. Come kill me tomorrow, or the day after, OK?"

Jack smiled in relief. "OK, I guess."

Two martini glasses containing a very cold white drink appeared on the counter. Unfiltered Sasanigori sake and Gzhelka vodka. A brine shrimp struggled at the bottom of each glass. Jack and Victor each took a drink in hand and placed their other hand on the back of the other man's neck. Each tipped his glass to the other's lips, and poured and drank, their foreheads touching as the sea monkeys died on their tongues.

On the street, Victor hailed a cab; Jack wandered. He let himself drift on the currents that wended through the downtown ecosystems but was barely aware of what he saw—the lush vegetation of the Chinese produce markets, the packs of predatory suits finished with the day's kill and looking for mates, restaurants that had so recently bubbled up from cracks in the city's crust that they still steamed and smoked with primordial heat—he was too distracted by his own voice screaming in his head, *Jack, you fucked up! Someone is going to kill you! You are going to die!* Because it seemed likely that he was. Victor, a former assassin and his unkilled target, would probably do it. Sure. Basic survival dictated it. Or the Elders would have him killed for not killing Victor. Why not? What good is an agent who won't execute his mission, especially when his mission is an execution?

Without quite knowing how he'd gotten there, Jack was back in the confines of the Lower East Side reef system, and soon he found himself standing in front of the battered red-steel-bomb-shelter door.

Pint of dark in hand, Jack surveyed the bar. The desperate faces, the aggressively neglected personal hygiene and attire, the representatives of type—biker, squatter, lawyer, thief, punk, pimp, librarian, drummer, junkie, novelist, swindler, bookie, kindergarten teacher—were still there, demographically the same, though individually different. Jack recognized no one until his gaze fell on the Spinning Yo-Yo Mystics of Balthazar's kabal at their table in the back. He approached them tentatively, walking sideways like a crab until he stood a few feet behind Balthazar.

Without turning his head, the rabbi sniffed deeply and said, "I smell Fish—Parrot fish, bluefish, one fish, two fish, needle fish, gefilte fish, Filet-O-Fish, whole fish, fish balls, Fishamajig, Jack Fish, my friend, Jack, why do you hesitate? Sit! Your yo-yo is your membership card until you realize that you don't need one—that the yo-yo circle encompasses everyone. But that is a lesson for much later. Sit. Spin."

The seat next to Balthazar was open, so Jack took it and put his backpack on his lap. He timidly pulled out his green yo-yo. He wished he had remembered to practice, but he'd been so busy running around, with all the spying and stuff.

He put the loop around his finger and let the disc fall to the end of the string where it bounced, wobbled, and dangled limply. Jack twitched his finger to make it jump spastically, but it would not climb its string back to his waiting palm.

"Jack. What are you doing?" asked Balthazar.

"Um. Dog-walking?"

"No, Jack. What are you *going to do*? Do you *know*?"

"Oh. Mmm. I see," said Jack, who didn't.

"Do you?" asked Balthazar.

"Do I see?'

"Do you *know*? You do not. You are going do something, or you are not, but you have to make a choice. You cannot *not* choose. Inaction is action just as action is."

"Oh," said Jack. And he tried repeating it to see if he understood. "Inaction is action just as action is. *Is*?"

"Is. *Not* choosing is making the choice *not* to choose. You do not choose to choose. You must choose. Either you choose to choose, or by not choosing, you have chosen. So choose."

"Choose? Choose what?"

"Choose a choice. It is inevitable, so be mindful. You must choose a choice."

The yo-yo rebbe gave Jack a long, significant look, leaned in close and said, "One more thing. It's all in the wrist."

He beckoned to his disciples.

"Come. It is time."

As one, the yo-yo initiates rose, gathered around their sage, and left.

Jack sat alone at the table with the empty glasses and the overflowing ashtrays and finished his beer. One by one, the empty chairs migrated to more popular tables. When Jack

stood up, someone took his chair, too. He interpreted that as
a sign to leave, to go back to the safehouse, where someone
might already be waiting to kill him. Reluctantly, he shuffled
toward the door, not wanting to stay, not wanting to leave,
when he heard, "So I'm sliding around on these fucking fur
sheets. Fur sheets! Can you believe it? Fucking fur sheets,
tickling my ass and the back of my sack!" And there was
Johnny Belmont telling his story to a pale, frail thing he'd
pinned to the bar before she could escape to her friends with
a round of toxic margaritas.

"And you won't believe what happened next," Johnny
Belmont bellowed into her wincing, unhealthy, fearful face.

Jack stepped up real close and deadpanned, "Batman
jumped out of the armoire and fucked you up the ass?"

In the stunned moment it took Johnny Belmont to recognize the guy who'd trumped his story, the girl ducked under
his thick arm and escaped into the darkness and noise of the
bar beyond. When Jack's face clicked for Belmont, he
punched him in the shoulder and laughed.

"Jackie baby! Siddown! Howz it goin'?"

"It's going fine. Just fine," Jack said vaguely.

Mac had two pints in front of them before they saw him
coming. They raised their glasses, clinked, and sipped.

"That Chloe Mitosis is something, huh? What did I tell
you? Huh? Huh!?! Oh yeah! Nice going, man!" Johnny
Belmont insinuated broadly.

"She sure is. Her, uh, piece was brilliant, I thought." Jack
tried to keep the conversation arty. "What a statement."

"Statement? I'll make a brilliant statement about her
piece—She's hot as fuck! Let *me* get into her clamshell for a

while, damn! I'd flatline for her too! Talk about CPR! Whoa!"

Jack didn't want to talk about CPR. He said, "Yeah, well, thanks for the introduction anyway."

Johnny Belmont suddenly remembered Landis, the money and the threats of harm to his person. Cagily, he asked, "She hook you up?"

"With what?"

"What you wanted. She answer your question?"

"Not really. No." instinctively, Jack covered up. "But it was worth a shot."

Johnny Belmont pressed, "So you never found him?"

"Well I—" Jack caught himself. Why should he tell Johnny Belmont anything? "Him who?"

"Gotta drain the main vein. Back in a minute!" Johnny Belmont hopped off his barstool and made for the can.

Jack didn't want to be there when Johnny Belmont got back. He was about to go when Mac dropped off two more pints "on the house!" Jack knew it would be terrible bar etiquette to eschew them, so he finished the beer he was working on and started in on the fresh one.

Johnny Belmont returned. "Drink up! I wanna take you somewheres."

"No, I mean, thanks, but I'd better be going."

"Where?"

Jack thought about more cable and leftovers at the safehouse. So he said, "OK."

Johnny Belmont smiled. "That's better. Drink up. We don't want to miss the show."

Johnny Belmont led Jack up the steps of the concrete loading dock of a former meat-packing warehouse. He kicked the heavy steel-jacketed door four times. It opened. Belmont pushed through a slashed curtain of plastic sheeting and Jack hit a wall of sound, smoke, and smells—they were in the Under Toad. Johnny Belmont joked with the man with the tattooed face who was working the door, then turned to Jack.

"Ten bucks a head—there's no list tonight." Jack peeled off four fives. The man stamped them and they passed under a blacklight. A glowing purple harpy looked up at Jack from the back of his wrist. He pushed aside another plastic curtain and found himself at the fringe of a heaving crowd, part of the outermost circle of the concentric rings defined by the bylaws of the subculture subscribing to tonight's genre:

Mean Chick Rock. The huge room was windowless, and hot. The concrete floor had patchy dark stains and drains in it to carry the blood away. The PA blasted Lydia Lunch.

"Good. We're here in time. They haven't gone on yet."

"Who hasn't gone on yet?"

Instead of answering the question, Johnny Belmont asked, "Thirsty?" And then he wandered off, presumably to get Jack something to drink.

Jack kept rooted to the same spot on the floor, trying to look like that was where he was supposed to be more than anywhere else, but he couldn't pull it off. He wobbled. His knees locked and he swayed. He fixed his gaze on a water stain on the ceiling. Then on a woman's leather-clad bottom three feet from where he was swaying, then back to the water stain in shame. He exhaled as if he had a lungful of cigarette smoke, even though he wasn't smoking.

As self-conscious as he felt, the people around him didn't seem to notice him. Mean Chick Nite pulled from a smear of subcultures, representing in their various uniforms. Suspenders-and-Docs ska chicks with short hair and rattails mashed it up with smiling-skull Motorhead leather-wearing Death-Dykes and a candy-colored posse of Fruits from Japan. A few dirty-dreaded Lalapoloozers hung with the neo-Mods with their jackets and skinny ties, and the couple of bona fide punks on the scene like Sailfish with pink and purple fins. Though there were as many men in the crowd as women, they somehow receded into the background. It was simply not their show, not their night for a change. And with the unleashed power of Woman in the room, it was fine with them.

Why am I here? Jack was already ready to leave. Hanging out with Johnny Belmont wasn't going to help him kill Victor Sargasso. Hanging out with Johnny Belmont wasn't even fun. It was not choosing a choice. Jack's hand pulled the yo-yo out of his pocket and with a little wrist-snap, let it fall and rise and caught it again. He looked at the round thing in his palm in surprise. Then something palpably changed in the atmosphere of the room. The lights were the same, the PA was still playing Lydia, but the herding instinct keyed the audience into focus. Like barracuda schooling for the hunt, people watched, waited, their awareness whirred, they went from being individuals collected from wherever they came from to the crowd that was *here* to *rock*. The Sirens took the stage, and without any word or sign they simultaneously struck a chord that hit Jack with the force of the tide in the Bay of Fundy. People screamed. The house lights went out, and tight white spots lit the band—three tall women in white vinyl breakaway jumpsuits and black Velvet Underground shades. The bass player was blonde, the guitarist was black, and the drummer Samoan. The formlessness of their uniforms only accentuated their individual differences and formidable inherent hotness. And then Miki Mu arrived.

Five feet tall in her bare feet, she was six feet tall in her shiny white platform boots. Her black hair was sticking out of the top of her head in two bunches, like fountains of shimmery spray. She wore a white leather coat and shades that matched the band's and she came out on the attack, singing in a voice that would have kept Ulysses going for another decade:

I got you right where I want you
Ain't no way you'll sail away
Gonna run you right up on my rocks
Sink you in my hole (down, down, down)
I got you right where I want you, baby
Ain't no way you'll sail away

It's Scylla or Charybdis
Either way you're going down
Scylla or Charybdis baby
Either way, you're going down

With a tear of Velcro, the band's white suits fell away simultaneously. Underneath they wore silver short shorts and tank tops. Miki Mu whipped off her shades, revealing her beautifully large and wide-set eyes and Jack was sure of what he had suspected from the first moment he saw her—*she's one of us.* Then the drummer counted off four quick ones on her sticks, and the double-time mosh commenced. The crowd knew it was coming and celebrated its arrival with a vehement surge of release, heaving themselves forward to be closer to Miki Mu, climbing the backs of the people in front, slamming headfirst into the stage, spinning, flailing, falling. It was as if the club was dashing itself on the hazardous rocks, hurling itself down the treacherous whirlpool, tossing its crew around its fetid hold.

Jack was thrown to the floor in the first wave of violence, and he struggled to navigate the stomping, skanking, kicking legs and heavy footwear. He came to a clearing and stood up—in the middle of the pit, where he was swung by his arm in a circle and flung into the living wall-of-death that was marching toward him. Someone grabbed him by the back of his pants and heaved him up. His feet found purchase on a chest, a face and a head, and now he was swimming above the crowd, hundreds of hands pushing him toward the stage, toward Miki Mu, who was in mid-spin with her mike stand raised and which she brought slamming into Jack's face as he horizontally arrived.

Jack hit the floor in a spectacular spray of droplets of his own blood, and was swiftly kicked in the kidneys and balls by three or four steel-toed boots. Jack had to move from that place. He started crawling.

He made it to the wall, and the relative sanctuary of being behind the focus of the crowd. He stood, panting and bleeding for a song-and-a-half before he realized the guy next to him was Johnny Belmont.

"Johnny Belmont!" Jack swatted him on the shoulder to get his attention.

Johnny Belmont did his best to act like Jack's whereabouts for the past half hour had been his chief concern, but the truth was that he had convinced himself that he was out alone.

"Where the hell did you go?" Belmont demanded. Without waiting for a response, he announced, "I already drank your beer, and mine too! Let's get some more!"

Johnny Belmont grabbed Jack's arm and pulled him toward a spiral staircase that led to a balcony and bar. Going up was made difficult by the occasional body tumbling down, but a combination of climbing, dodging, and stepping on people brought them to the upper level. He guided Jack to a

pair of empty stools overlooking the balcony and then vanished, reappearing moments later armed with beer.

"You look like shit!" said Johnny Belmont. Jack knew he
was right.

Jack's nose was swollen, crusty, and still bleeding a bit.
His architect clothes were soaked, torn, and smeared with
filth. There were cigarette butts in his hair. His shoes were
untied. His body was bruised, and all the soft parts hurt. He
smiled at Johnny Belmont and said, "Fuck you. You're
drunk," which was true, as it nearly always was.

From this vantage point, the scene below was no less
chaotic. In fact, the perspective afforded context, and this
made each violent act, absurd gesture, and spontaneous
exultation even more disturbing. A girl, no more than fifteen, wearing a black wonderbra and jeans tucked into pink
snowboarding boots ran up beside Jack. She sported a full-
back tattoo depicting the gates of hell. In one fluid motion
she vaulted over the balcony rail, and spread-eagled, flew
out over the crowd, to be caught and supported by a thicket
of upraised hands.

"Dee-amn, I'd let her assassinate me with *that* little ass!"
Johnny Belmont proclaimed, staring hard at Miki Mu.

"What? What do you mean?" There was something
about the way Belmont said *assassinate* that Jack liked even
less then the way Belmont said *ass*.

"Huh? Oh. I mean look at her—tight little body, fuckin'
gorgeous hair, those eyes—a night with her would *kill* me,
kill me, I tell ya!"

Jack reluctantly admitted to himself that Belmont had a
point: Miki Mu was outrageously lethal-looking. She had so

much presence and power that it couldn't be contained in her small person. It surrounded her in an electric aura, beamed from her sharp eyes and poured from her throat as she sang. Jack was transfixed and afraid.

For the next forty minutes, the Sirens pounded out an uninterrupted set of heroic, potent, buoyant, cruel, and heartbreaking songs from their new record, *Bimini Road*. Miki Mu took the crowd on a sonic journey through sea changes of mood and time that only Jack could really understand. She sang of Cleito and her love for Poseidon ("Build You a Temple"), war with Athens ("Gonna Fuck You Up if it Brings Me Down"), and the long centuries of living alone at the bottom of the sea ("Living Alone at the Bottom of the Sea"). The Sirens were "tighter than clams with lockjaw," as Johnny Belmont elegantly put it.

The band came on like a hurricane. Each song gathered moisture and strength from the crowd, dessicating them, until the club was filled with an evil green howling wind. Then the hurricane's blue eye opened to bathe the crowd with sunlight, until the second storm front hit, more tremendous than before, whirling around and around the room on Miki Mu's voice, on the inexorable pounding of the bass and drums, the piercing wail of the guitar. Bodies flew through the air; the furniture was smashed to pieces.

When the set finally ended, Miki Mu said from the floor, where she lay on her back, spent, finished, done, "It's over. That's all we've got. Angora Fuzz is next."

Jack was wiped out. His entire lifetime underwater had been compressed into three-quarters of an hour of the most intense music he'd ever heard. Johnny Belmont was ecstatic.

"Oh, man. That was incredible, and now the Fuzz! I love the Fuzz! My former colleagues! Yeah—the best part is they really are cops! No—the best part is they really are lesbians! Lesbian cops! *That* is the best part! That they really are lesbian cops!" Johnny Belmont laughed for a bit before he began choking.

With the sounds of an approaching helicopter thudding out of the PA, Angora Fuzz took the stage. They wore Kevlar vests and blue thongs and big stomping riot boots. Lieutenant Anger Lopez Wright sang:

> *Fourteen hours in my car,*
> *I know where the bastards are,*
> *Can't fucking bust 'em—got no cause,*
> *I can't break the fucking laws,*

The music dropped out, and everyone in the room who wasn't Jack or Johnny Belmont shouted:

> *By God I'm gonna break their jaws!*

Officer Linda Phoenicia spun her guitar around her neck, and nailing a power chord, brought the tune into the chorus:

> *Stakeout!*
> *Piss in a cup.*
> *Stakeout!*
> *My shift is up.*
> *Stakeout!*
> *Fuck the DA.*

Stakeout
Ain't no fucking way
to be The Man.

A chant began on stage and spilled into the crowd until the room pumped with hundreds of voices who proclaimed as one:

I Am the Man!
I Am the Man!
I Am the Man!
I Am the Man!

Jack heard the voice again, this time quite close, the voice that could lure him to death on a rocky coast, keep him from ever going back to Penelope. She was standing right next to him—Miki Mu. He was sure she was going to kill him.

"Is this Fish?" she asked Johnny Belmont.

"That's Fish," Belmont confirmed.

She looked at Jack's nose and shook her head.

"That's what happens when you get too close to my stage, Fish."

"I Ii," said Jack, holding up three fingers in the Trident Salute. She looked at him hard for a moment, and said to Johnny Belmont, "Go. Get me a drink, wouldja?"

Belmont nodded and dutifully went to the bar.

Miki took his stool and leaned in close to Jack. She pointed to a tattoo on her left biceps—a trident, like his, only solid black.

"I assume you know what this means."

Jack did know, and he also knew what the three inter-locked bracelets that jangled and clinked on her right wrist—one of bronze, one of tin, and one of the Atlantean glowing red metal orichalcum—were about. Miki Mu was more than the lead Siren. She was also an Orichalcum Guardian, the Right Prong of the Trident, an elite warrior, an assassin, and not somebody he wanted to encounter in the middle of a mission. Jack knew that she was up here to kill somebody. He prayed to Poseidon that it wasn't him.

She put her hand on his shoulder, friendly-like. "So, where is he? You can still save yourself if you bring me to him."

Jack knew it was hopeless, but tried to pretend he didn't know whom she was talking about. "What? Who?" he stammered.

Miki Mu knew Jack knew whom she was talking about and kept going like she did. "Come on! It'll be fun," she said. "We'll kill him together. That would be good for you, you know."

Jack knew he shouldn't, but he snapped, "He works for a big firm using his own name. Did you really need me to come up here and tell you where to find him?"

Miki Mu squeezed, not hard, but accurately, pinching a nerve that paralyzed Jack's right side. She brought her face close to Jack's. "Victor Sargasso knows me from something we did together a few years ago. That's why you had to find him, and why you were supposed to kill him. Since you did-n't, you will now bring me to him. He sees you first and I kill him, easy." She smiled. "He won't be on his guard since you jellied out the first time you were supposed to whack him."

Jack was slowly getting it. "Johnny Belmont told you I found Sargasso."

"Johnny Belmont owes Landis a sum he'll never have in one place. Johnny Belmont wants me to like him so I don't kill him, and because I'm hot. Let me tell you something about Johnny Belmont: You can trust Johnny Belmont as long as you're trusting Johnny Belmont to do what's best for Johnny Belmont. Understand?

"I think I do now."

"So?"

Belmont came back with three vodka tonics. He saw the expression on Jack's face and said, "Look, I had to tell her. I had to make sure they knew. I don't have the money, so I had to make sure they had the information."

"Yeah, sure," said Jack out of the left side of his mouth.

"I think you just settled your account with Landis," Miki said to Johnny Belmont.

Belmont smiled, showing his eroded teeth. "Pleasure doing business with you. Let me know if I can ever help out again."

"Oh, we will. Now go away."

Johnny Belmont stood there, drink in hand, leering.

"Not a chance, Johnny," Miki Mu laughed.

Johnny Belmont snorted and slapped Jack on the shoulder, causing him to bounce funny. Then he downed his drink in three gulps and set out on his never-ending search for pussy.

Miki Mu stared at Jack, idly stirring her drink but not drinking it. Jack grew more and more uncomfortable, especially because the right half of his body was paralyzed.

When she felt that Jack was on the edge, Miki Mu asked, "Where is he now?"

Jack should have told her, but he didn't. He wasn't sure why. It went against his training as an Agent, his education as an Atlantean, his loyalty to the Elders, and his ambitions as a spy.

"He's up to something," he said, without much conviction.

"What do you mean?"

"Release me and I'll tell you."

Miki Mu smiled and gave his nipple a twist. His right arm twitched and flopped and a shiver ran up and down his body. He shook it off and took a squirt of his cocktail through the tiny straw. It was strong, acerbic medicine that went straight to his brain. Jack felt his eyes open; he saw things with enhanced resolution as the cocktail burned through some of the stray thoughts between relevant pieces of information and he realized that Sargasso *was* up to something.

He leaned back in his stool and said, "Right after I located him, I was picked up by the Maltese and told that I *couldn't* find him. Why?"

"Yeah, why?"

"If we kill him now, we'll never know. I think we should wait. If he's doing a deal with the Maltese, the Elders would want to know, wouldn't they? A rogue Agent is one thing, but a Maltese plot, well, that's something else."

"Maybe. And maybe the Elders already know all this and want him dead before he does the thing he's planning to do."

"Give me one more day. I'll find out what I can."

"And how are you going to do that?"

"I got myself a job at Triton, where Sargasso works. I'll go back tomorrow and see what I can find out."

"All right, Fish." She smiled. "You get your day."

Angora Fuzz were now into their encore, "Bad Cop/Worse Cop." The exhausted audience summoned up their fight or flight adrenaline reserves and gave the final mosh a primal effort. Anger Lopez Wright patrolled the edge of the stage, kicking anyone who attempted to enter her zone. The audience screamed the chorus along with Lieutenant Wright:

> *Bad Cop Worse Cop what's the fuckin' dif?*
> *Liberal judge paroled another punk-ass little*
> *   shit.*
> *War on crime! War on crime! Here comes*
> *   your fucking war!*
> *Bad cop's getting worse this time, and worse*
> *   cop's getting more! More! More! More!*
> *Up against the wall! Up against the wall!*
> *(Motherfucker)*
> *Up*
> *Against*
> *The fuckin'*
> *Wall!*

Miki Mu was gone, Johnny Belmont was gone, Jack had no reason to be there anymore, and still he sat at the table sipping through the tiny straw until the band had packed up their stuff, the houselights were on, and the sound guy was mopping the floor.

At seven in the morning, people were already at work at Triton Architecture. Jack walked through reception with his reading glasses blurring the horrible view, and continued right past his desk. He skirted the materials library in case Conrad was in early and found Heather balancing an unstable ziggurat of papers and chipboard models so tall it blocked her face. Jack swept in and pulled the top half of the pile off. "Let me help you with this."

"Thanks," said Heather, peering down at Jack. She was almost a full head taller than him. And gorgeous, with angular cheekbones and a fabulous Jil Sander black suit. Her eyes narrowed with suspicion. "Who are you?" she asked, then added, "Walk with me. There's no time."

Jack hurried behind her explaining, "I'm the new intern.

I got stuck with Gordon in E&I doing bathrooms, but Conrad said I could talk to you about moving to E&E."

Heather walked very quickly toward the conference rooms in the middle of the floor. She had incredible posture and a long stride, and Jack had to skip to keep up with her. She spoke to Jack over her shoulder.

"We're extremely busy. No time to train you," she said. "I don't know. . ."

"Don't even think about it," Jack offered. "My day doesn't start for two hours. I'll help you set up for your presentation. Maybe we can talk about it later."

"Fine," Heather agreed. "Get the door."

Jack put the papers and models down on a file cabinet and opened the door. Heather pushed in front of him, set her load on the glass table, and began organizing piles. Without looking up she said, "Go back to my desk. There's a big model on the table behind it. Bring it over."

"Sure," Jack said, but his feet didn't move. There was a large, color drawing pinned to the wall, a schematic plan for a theme park to be built in Neptune, New Jersey. Jack didn't need to read the text to know what it was—the shape alone told him everything, and it also told him why Victor Sargasso should die.

Three rings of water surrounded three rings of land, like a dartboard. Jack knew that shape—it was the shape of the place where Jack had grown up, gone to spy school, and been sent away on his first mission. It was the shape of the Royal Metropolis of Atlantis, built by Poseidon for his bride, Cleito, and now home to the Council of Elders and the remnants of what had been the earth's greatest civilization. Its location was beyond secret—that it was by its very nature hidden had been the unquestioned basis of everything Atlantean for thousands of years. But to even acknowledge its form was punishable by the slowest death devisable by the Guardians. And here it was, in full color and mounted on foamcore, with various iconographic temples scattered on the land and phallic dolphins cavorting in the water, ready for presentation to the clients at ten o'clock.

"I need that model," Heather reminded Jack. "Hurry!"

Jack retreated to the Entertainment and Exhibition studio to collect the model. It was a sort of diorama made from the drawing he had seen in Chloe's studio—Poseidon's temple with its herd of bulls was mounted behind a mini version of the statue of the sea god holding the blowfish. Jack felt dead inside. He picked the thing up and held it facing forward so he wouldn't have to look at it.

There was worse already in the conference room. Images from Chloe's sketchbook had been adapted and blown up and pinned to the walls—jagged pyramids sported water-slides, temples and chapels housed rest rooms and cafés and souvenir stands. There were Sphinxes and Chaac heads and fish on spears all over the place. One wall was labeled GROUNDMAKING. Pinned to it was an enlarged photo of Chloe clad in her muslin robe. There was also an illustration of a golden shovel, along with a list of dignitaries, including the Mayor of Neptune, some state senators, and a former Miss New Jersey, and the date, which Jack noted with alarm, was tomorrow.

Jack took a long look at the mammoth schematic drawing and he couldn't help smiling. With Chloe's help, Sargasso had designed the ultimate bastardized fantasy Atlantis, using bits of all the lore and nonsense that had been floated from the Ministry of Information to wash up where it could be found by susceptible weirdoes. The islands were dotted with fake temples and chariot go-kart racetracks and bumperboat domes. The innermost water ring was to be stocked with sharks and rays and synthetic coral to be viewed from a table in the sunken, glass-walled food court. On the bottom-right corner of the plan, the name of the project and the client's name were printed in blue—ATLANTISLAND, it read, NEPTUNE, NJ, PREPARED FOR MALTA KNIGHTS, SA. Jack's smile flattened and died.

There was a stack of takeaway/leavebehind PowerPoint decks on the table that had the schematic on the cover page. Jack took one when Heather had her back turned.

"I don't know how he does it," Heather was saying.

"What? I mean, who? Does what?" Jack asked.

"Victor. I mean, his work is always inspired, but this time, I mean, it's visionary. Honestly, it's a strange project. The client is willing to spend anything, they love all of Victor's ideas, and they keep asking for more."

"More? More what?" Jack really wanted to know.

"More everything. More detail, more rides, more build-ings, more *everything*." She pointed to the big plan. "When Victor showed them the layout with the concentric islands, I've never seen a client so excited. The partners here were sure they would reject it as too expensive, I mean, digging those huge moats, and in Jersey with mob construction and all the environmental crap to deal with, but they loved it, they approved it all."

"Yeah," said Jack. "I bet they did." As Heather was speaking, Jack was studying the plan, and he saw that Sargasso's sellout went deeper than pyramids and dolphins. Every important bureau, building, school, and ministry in Atlantis had an amusement doppelgänger on Victor's map. For a map was precisely what it was, to someone who wanted to navigate the Hidden City.

"There you are!" exclaimed an exfoliated Gordon from the doorway. "Where the hell are my drawings?"

Jack spent the morning with a dog-eared AutoCAD manual in his lap. It was in Dutch, presumably the first language of the previous occupant of Jack's cubicle, but not a tongue he had learned in spy school. He was trying to reformat a drawing of a men's room for the Schneider Schnitzel factory in Stuttgart. Every few minutes, Gordon's shiny face would swoop down over Jack's shoulder, chiding him, "Metric, Jack. The stall doors have to be metric!"

By the time Jack managed to get away from Gordon, Sargasso and the whole Entertainment & Exhibitions team was at the Oyster Bar with the clients. He tried to sneak back into the conference room to find out more about what was going on in Neptune, but the door wouldn't open. After trying and failing to pick the lock, snapping the metal tip off his compass, Jack decided that he knew enough. He put on his reading glasses and headed for the elevators.

J ack racewalked across 59th Street as the light changed against him, dodged around the glossy-loined horses and anachronistic carriages, and plunged into the leafy corner of Central Park. His feet got the nervous message to hurry and skipped into a light run—past the caricature artists, the Nuts 4 Nuts pushcart, the tame squirrels and the international tourists feeding them nuts from the pushcart they were nuts for. He was a few minutes late to meet Miki Mu at the Zoo and he was tense. At best, being late was rude, and with her, he thought it might even be fatal.

Jack flashed his membership card and the burly Latina in green polyester waved him through the turnstile. He had no problem finding the Sea Lions—their octagonal pool was the centerpiece of the main courtyard. He was having some trouble breathing though, and he had to lean against the metal rail that surrounded the pool to get his wheezing under control. If it exploded into hacking and he jumped into the water to cure it, his cover would be blown.

A small crowd had gathered at the far end of the exhibit: a group of parochial school girls in plaid jumpers chaperoned by a stern black woman holding an umbrella and a megaphone; five women talking on cell phones and pushing sleeping toddlers in strollers; an Orthodox Jewish couple with six children—three incrementally smaller male analogs of their father in identical plain black suits, and three girlish versions of their mother wearing long denim skirts, and white blouses; assorted divorced fathers on their weekly outing with the offspring of failed first marriages, looking for new wives half the age of the old ones; a college couple on a cheap date after wake-up sex and breakfast on the meal plan; and a courier wearing a messenger bag and bike helmet, waiting idly for runs downtown. Jack anxiously looked around. Miki Mu wasn't where she'd said she would be, sitting on the steps, waiting for the show to start.

Three pretty and professional-looking women in khaki uniforms and knee-high rubber boots came marching through the crowd swinging stainless steel pails.

"Coming through!"

"Please leave the center aisle clear!"

"The feeding is about to begin!"

On the rocky artificial island in the middle of the pool, three sleek dark shapes awakened with yelps and barks and slipped into the water. They swam excitedly around the island, their wake spilling water into the dry moat surrounding the tank. Jack could smell why. Mackerel, herring, sardines—those buckets were full of the good stuff. He salivated.

The three keepers crossed the rocky footbridge to the island, where they took up their positions. Three foxy women in brown uniforms and rubber boots with buckets of fish and pouty looks. *Damn*, thought Jack, *this zoo is hot!* A volunteer wearing blue picked up a microphone and faced the crowd. She said her name was Judy and she explained that *The show is as much for the benefit of the animals as it is for your entertainment.* There was some light applause.

After a flurry of hand signals from their keepers, the three sea lions popped out of the water and took their assigned positions on the island. Judy introduced the animals and their respective handlers: Breezy with Melba; April with Marisol; and Scooter with Trixie, the new keeper who was making her zoo debut.

The ladies flicked fish to the sea lions, who shook hands, turned in circles, swam around the island, gave kisses, and bellowed on command. Melba had the most outgoing sea lion—the crowd favorite—but it was Trixie who had Jack's attention. She had the least cooperative animal and was valiantly playing off what was a very good example of how not to train a sea lion to do anything. Scooter was in the water when the others were on the rocks, on the rocks when the others were in the water. He blew kisses for laughs while Trixie helplessly shouted commands. She finally picked up her bucket and turned her back on her charge, who wriggled on his belly and whined in apology.

Jack felt a sharp poke in his kidney.

"You must like waking up in Dumpsters, Fish," whispered a throaty voice. Then Miki Mu laughed and said, "You'd better pay more attention. Maltese woulda spiked you before you knew they were there. Come on." And without waiting for Jack, she walked up the stairs toward the Penguin House. Jack took one last look at Trixie, who was trying to coax her submerged charge out of the water by shaking a sardine a few inches above his snout.

The Penguin House was full—full of penguins and of people looking at them. Behind thick glass, the birds waddled around on their concrete ice floe, building nests of polished black stones, sitting on eggs real and dummy, and swimming around the watery part of their habitat in their funny penguin formal wear. On the near side of the glass, a grammar school class from the Bronx—a shoal of beautiful brown and black and gold children in blue-and-white uniforms—was being scolded by women with lisps and long nails. The air itself was full of sharp, bright sounds—the endlessly looping recording of a penguin colony during mating season and the strident yelps of glee, injustice, and wonder from the crowd of children.

Jack waded through the knots of kids toward a bench at the back of the viewing theater and sat down next to Miki Mu. He ran his hand across the carpeted wall and started to speak, but Miki Mu stuck her palm in his face. Her eyes were on two penguins engaged in a furious chase, first swiftly through the water, then awkwardly across the concrete beach then—*plop plop*—back into the water again, and around and around.

"Reminds me of my ex," Miki Mu chuckled.

"Are you sure it's okay to talk here?" Jack whispered hoarsely.

Miki Mu pointed to the nearest kid who was clutching a plastic bottle of Hawaiian Punch. "You're right. Kid could be working for anyone—probably has a tape recorder in that bottle. Better not let him overhear us!"

Then she grew serious and asked quietly, "*What*?"

"He's doing something big—a theme park in New Jersey. with the same layout as the Royal Metropolis. The Knights are paying for it."

"Why would a bunch of crusading sardine importers want to build an amusement park in New Jersey?"

Jack shrugged, venturing, "Everybody loves a good flume?"

At the back of the penguin exhibit, a door opened in the ersatz Antarctic sky. Trixie, holding a clipboard, stepped carefully onto the concrete ice floe. A male keeper with earrings and two steel fish pails trailed behind her.

"True. But something else is going on. Is it real or just a proposal?"

"No, they're actually building something. There's a groundbreaking ceremony tomorrow."

"*Crabs*! OK, Fish. He must really have it."

"The—" But Miki Mu had her hand over Jack's mouth before he could say, *Star*.

Miki Mu glared at Trixie, who was glaring right back, oblivious to greedy Spike, who had already had his vitamin-enhanced fish and was sneaking another herring out of her hand. The male keeper said something to Trixie and she resumed her feeding duties, while glancing at Jack and

Miki Mu out of the corner of her eye. Jack saw that Trixie was tragically inept at her job. Spike bit her on the ass, then waddled through her legs and cut back into the food line for thirds.

"Funny little guys, huh? Let's go see the polar bears," Miki Mu suggested, looking warily at Trixie. "Sometimes they give 'em frozen chickens full of chocolate syrup. They just rip the fuckers apart and their mouths turn all brown."

The polar bears were not, as it turned out, eating chocolate-filled chickens. They were sleeping—Gus in his cave, Ida and Lilly on the bluff above. Jack and Miki Mu stood behind the plate glass screen overlooking the polar bears' swimming area. In the reflection of the glass, Jack saw the faintest glint of gold. The blur resolved itself into Trixie, and Jack fell to the ground in a rolling-into-the-bushes defensive move. Miki Mu kick-flipped backwards off the glass screen and seized Trixie by her brown canvas belt. Trixie's Latin-jabbering walkie-talkie and her gold breech-loading tranquilizer gun clattered to the ground as Miki Mu lifted the larger woman above her head and heaved her over the screen to plunge into the polar bears' play-pond.

Great, white slumbering Gus lifted his head with interest at the splash and loped toward the new plaything introduced into his environment. Peering through the glass below the waterline, the kids from the Bronx were surprised and delighted to suddenly see a zookeeper before them, thrashing her arms and legs in the pool. Somewhere an alarm went off, and the dull thumping of rubber boots running on pavement approached from all directions.

"We're going to that ceremony," Miki Mu hissed. "We

leave tonight. Rendezvous at midnight under the leaky rowboat at the Thai place on North Seventh. Now go!" She shoved Jack toward the Snow Monkey house and, slipping through a khaki scrum of panicked zookeepers, she was gone.

Jack pulled the tray of soggy fishsticks from the microwave and winced. With the cornucopia of the city all around it, the safehouse freezer was stocked exclusively with Deep-C products in an attempt to make the Agents feel at home. Jack didn't want to feel at home. He would feel at home only if he made it back home. While he was up in the Topworld, he wanted to savor every new flavor he could.

There was a lit cigarette in his hand that Jack didn't recall lighting. He dragged on it, coughed, and threw it in the toilet when he passed the bathroom on his looping path through the apartment. Jack realized that he had been pacing the three rooms in an elongated figure eight for some time. He had no idea how long. On his next pass through the kitchen, Jack glanced at the clock. He had a couple of hours before the meeting under the boat, before going to New Jersey, before violent danger, killing, and—Jack stopped himself again. This is where he kept winding up in his head, getting hurt, screaming, dying in various horrible ways, descending into hypothetical scenarios of fear, panic, and black pain.

No, Jack attempted self-discipline. *Review the mission so far.* He had been trained to do this: he might have missed something crucial, or made a mistake that could still be remedied. Jack took a bottle of Evian from the fridge, shot a jet up his nostril, and told himself to calm down.

He tried to play back everything he'd done since hitting the beach at Coney Island, but no matter where he started, he would hear Johnny Belmont telling the Batman story. When he was able to make it stop, he would quickly fast-forward or rewind to the Chloe parts—meeting her at the diving-board bar, watching her perform, rolling with her into the pool. *She couldn't know what was really going on, it had to be just a job to her, right?* Just a job, like it was Jack's job to kill her ex-boyfriend and stop a Maltese plot to steal secrets or a sacred Star.

Jack stopped pacing. He would warn her; there was still time. Jack went to the kitchen and pulled another Ziploc from the box. Then he changed his mind and put it back. His eyes were finally healing. This time he would walk.

Jack crouched behind a brown Datsun 280 ZX and peered across its long hood. He was at the edge of the ad hoc parking lot on Manhattan Avenue in front of the artists' factory space, watching Chloe and the bald guy from the pool, whose name, he overheard, was Clive. They were tying down a pair of six-foot claws to the roof rack of a rusted-out Rabbit GTI with bungie cords. The car was parked by the factory loading dock, the back stuffed with boxes and bags, the folded blue gowns and the golden bowl that Jack had seen in Chloe's studio. Jack was watching from behind the car because he saw that someone else was watching too—the black GNX that had chased the DickVan up and down Coney Island Avenue was parked opposite the Rabbit across the street with two Goldties inside. It confirmed what Jack had come to tell Chloe—that she was in danger, that the combination of a rogue Agent, the Maltese, an Orichalcum Guardian, and the Mayor of Neptune would add up to disaster, that she should stay away from the "groundmaking" ceremony with her robes and her claws and her golden bowl. He wanted to walk over and tell her everything, but knew that if the Maltese saw him, they'd kill him on sight or capture him and take him to Gozo and then kill him. Jack decided that he needed a new plan.

The parking lot was used by a lot of people other than the artists and artisans from the factories. Car service drivers used it for napping, crackheads used it for their five-dollar blowjob businesses, and kids used it to party and throw things into the Creek. A member of one of these groups had left behind a screw-top bottle that had once held forty ounces of Old English 800 and now held the same quantity of malt liquor after being filtered through his kidneys. The bottle sat next to Jack by the front fender of the 280Z, and he picked it up and took it with him as he began slowly worming his way around to the back of the Buick.

"Shit! I forgot my tail," Jack heard Chloe yell to Clive. "I'll be right back!"

Crawl, crawl, scurry, roll, crouch, crawl, lie flat. Jack was under one of the Buick's two silent mufflers now. He didn't know how cars worked, but he figured that if he took off his shirt, ripped it into quarters, soaked them in a puddle, balled them up, and shoved them into the four tailpipes, it would have an adverse effect on the car's performance. Jack took off his shirt, ripped it into quarters, soaked them in a puddle, balled them up, and shoved them into the tailpipes. Then he rolled out and inched forward very slowly until he crouched alongside the rear tire on the passenger side. In the frenzy of tuning and detailing the GNX, the Maltese had elected to replace the stock chrome gas cap with a much classier gold-plated model. Jack quietly unscrewed it and tipped the bottle of pee into the open throat of the fuel pipe. Then he unscrewed the gold-plated cap to the tire stem and depressed the pin in the center with a quarter. *Woosh!* The air came screaming out of the Goodyear Eagle, the loudest sound that Jack had ever heard. *Woooosh!* It kept coming with no discernible effect on the tire. *Woooooooosh!* Finally, the blast of air diminished and the hindquarters of the car sat down hard on the fat rim. Jack squeezed the pin as hard as he could and kept squeezing even when he heard the passenger door open. Still holding the pin down, Jack flung his body around and kicked the Goldtie in the shins, faceplanting him onto the tarmac.

Sudden, tremendous pain in his wrist made Jack's hand leap off the stem and drop the quarter. The driver had gotten out, come around the back of the car, and hit Jack with The Club. Jack rolled away and managed to get to his feet only to be tackled from behind and brought down again. His hand found the empty OE bottle and he hurled it blindly. He was rewarded with a crash and a grunt of pain. Jack kicked back hard and scrambled forward in a desperate run for the Rabbit. Chloe was hopping down from the loading dock.

"Get out of here!" Jack yelled in warning. "Go! Drive! Go!"

"What the fuck?" Chloe saw Jack barreling toward her, shirtless and bleeding, followed by two pissed-off-looking guys in black suits.

"Clive!" Chloe called as she opened the driver's door and stuffed in her tail. "Stalker! Glove compartment! Mace!"

"Neptune!" Jack yelled, running toward her. "Danger! Don't go!"

Chloe was in the car, rolling up her window and working the ignition. It coughed and scraped before catching. Clive was out his window, leaning across the claws on the roof, pointing a canister at Jack and the Maltese.

"Neptune!" Jack shouted as he was tackled against Chloe's door. His face was only inches from hers on the other side of the glass. For an instant, they could see into each other's eyes, Jack's broadcasting deep concern and affection, Chloe's fright and disgust, until their connection was broken by Jack's head hitting her window.

Chloe hit the gas and the car lurched into gear. Clive let off a cloud of noxious spray as Jack and his attackers landed in a pile. The front wheels of the Volkswagen chirped, the empty canister clattered hollowly to the ground. One of the Maltese broke and ran for the GNX with tears and snot streaming from his face. The Buick grunted and sputtered and gasped before starting, then veered off sideways on its one good rear wheel. When the urine reached the cylinders the turbo units squealed in disgust and, choking on its own exhaust, the beast died quietly in the middle of the street.

Jack kicked and pushed his way free of the other Goldtie

and stumbled forward, crying blind. Head down, bent double, Jack staggered in the direction of the worst thing he could smell until he fell the last eight feet into the unctuous embrace of the Newtown Creek.

The Rabbit got away.

"What the hell happened to you, Fish?" Miki Mu asked, as Jack took a stool at the bar. Wet, shirtless, scraped and bloodied, eyes bloodshot, huge bruise on his forehead, stinking of the River, Jack smiled and said, "Sorry, ran into somebody I knew."

"'Sup?" Dick asked obliviously through a mouthful of Phuket dumpling.

It was difficult to hear in the cavernous room. With a twenty-five-foot ceiling and no surface made from any material softer than concrete, glass, or iron, the acoustics were terrible. The aluminum dinghy that hung from the ceiling dripping water from hundreds of holes into a Plexiglas cistern didn't help conversation either. Nor did the constant ringing in Jack's head.

"Am I late?" He saw the collection of Singha bottles and the remains of crabcakes and summer rolls on rectangular plates arrayed on the counter in front of Miki Mu and Dick. "Sorry," he apologized sheepishly.

"Dick, go get the DickVan. We'll meet you in front," ordered Miki Mu.

Dick slid off his stool and hurried away.

"Maltese?"

Jack nodded.

She shook her head. "C'mon, Fish. You were supposed to lie low. Now they know you know something."

They sat at the bar, staring straight ahead, listening to the sound of water draining out of a rowboat full of holes. A waiter came by and vibed them hard.

Miki Mu put eight fives on the bar.

"Neptune?" said Jack.

"Neptune, Fish," said Miki Mu. "With a coupla stops along the way."

The DickVan rolled up North Seventh, slowing down as it approached the Thai joint. The sliding door slid open. Miki Mu and Jack jumped in and bounced around on the fuckmat as the DickVan accelerated through a yellow light. Miki Mu called shotgun. Jack slammed the side door closed and she tossed him a fresh I ♥ NY T-shirt from the glove compartment. They were past Bedford, past Driggs, past Roebling, past the last outpost of the post-punk hipster-trendies, through the Italian reaches of the Northside and under the BQE heading into Polish Greenpoint.

"OK. When you're sure we don't have a gold tail, take us in for the pickup at Landis LIC," Miki Mu directed.

"Copy that," agreed Dick. "Jack, give me eyes in the back of my head."

"Uh, copy that," Jack replied, dragging the Igloo cooler to the back of the van and sitting on top of it. He touched the rude harpoon hole and felt the cool air sucked in by the swift passage of the DickVan. Through the grimy window he saw refracted headlights, the shadowy steel supports of the highway, grim clapboard houses looming in the grey night—no obvious threats.

"Any sardines?" Miki Mu called from the front.

"Uh, that's a negatory. All clear. No problemo—"

"OK, we get it. Just keep watching," admonished Miki Mu. Then she said, "*Go*," to Dick, who went.

He cut left, picked up McGuinness by the Key Food full of firemen and hauled ass over the Pulaski Bridge into Queens. Jack watched through the window and realized that he actually knew where he was, that the vast, inscrutable Topworld was in fact knowable, finite and real, at least in a tiny sliver. Then Dick skirted the mouth of the Midtown tunnel and drove along Vernon, and Jack was in another long, bleak stretch of an outer borough with no map, a lunatic at the wheel, and a killer in command. He jumped. Was that a gold Caprice swerving at them, getting into position for a harpoon shot? No, it was a yellow cab trying to get back to Manhattan as fast as possible after a one-way fare to Astoria and no tip.

"Let this guy go," Jack advised his pilot.

Dick took them past huge brown projects, brothers wearing

multiple hats and logo jackets and brand new sneakers, preening on the fences and steps out front. He took them past Italian bakeries and Greek kabob houses, under the R tracks, down avenues, streets, and roads bearing the same numbers, past hookers waiting for the pre-dawn prisoner release at Queens Plaza, past huge movie studios and tiny barber shops until Dick said, "Dick's lost!" and then "Aww shit, Dick knows were he is!" and they all held their breath as they went by the MaltaKnights Anchovy Warehouse with its roll-up door open a few feet off the ground and a guy with a mustache smoking a cigar and reading the *Post* on a broken swivel chair on the sidewalk out front.

They were getting close to the Pool Supply showroom.

"All right. I want you to roll by. If it looks clear we'll get out a block away. You go around back and wait for us. Keep the door open, this has to be fast. Then we get out of town."

"We taking the Lincoln?"

"No, the George."

They did it the way Miki Mu said. They drove slowly up the block with the newsstand and the diner and the A.T. Landis Pool Supply Showroom and Warehouse and looked inside. The lights were on, and Jack could see Flo behind the counter talking to a customer. Miki Mu and Jack slid the side door open and rolled out of the DickVan at ten miles per hour. Dick accelerated once they were on the ground and turned at the next corner. Jack and Miki Mu crossed the street.

"If someone sees us, do you think we should start making out so they think we're like lovers out for a stroll?" Jack asked hopefully.

"No," Miki Mu said. "Nice try, though."

Inside the store, a white guy with no socks and a fat wallet was comparing skimmers. As he telescoped them out and whipped them around, Flo said to Miki and Jack, "I'll be with you in a minute," and nodded her head significantly. While No Socks Skimmer Guy narrowed down his choices, Jack and Miki perused the Jacuzzi scrapers. Flo discreetly picked up the phone, touched a button and said into the receiver, "Bob? Could you pack up that order for New Jersey?"

No Socks Skimmer Guy finally chose the Landis Extendo-Reach II, paid with Platinum, and took it out to his Range Rover. Jack and Miki followed Flo to the back room.

Bob was zipping up a long ski bag.

"Here's everything you asked for: The triple-band gun, the carbon railgun and the OMER pneumatic, the 6 millimeter spinner rock tips, the 7 millimeter 5-prong galvanized tips, the .357 powerheads. Everything's fletched and modified for air use. You've got enough points in here to stop a humpback."

Miki nodded. "We're going to need umbrellas," she said. "Big ones."

"Right," said Bob, "*um*brellas." He went to a closet and took out three oversized, white golf umbrellas emblazoned with the CHLORINATOR POOL SHOCK logo. Miki put them in the open ski bag and zipped it. Jack picked up the other one, and they started for the back door. Jack hesitated. He stepped over to Bob and in a quiet voice asked, "Do you have a spare mankini? I, uh, lost mine."

"Flo? Do we have any more mankinis?" Bob bellowed. "He looks like a small!"

With the final piece of essential gear in hand, Flo opened

the back door and there was the DickVan, its side door open wide. They tossed the bags onto the fuckmat, exchanged salutes with Flo and Bob and were off.

"Load up," said Miki Mu, opening her bag.

She took out the long aluminum speargun, screwed a spinner rock tip on a shaft, loaded it, and with some effort pulled back the three giant rubber bands. She handed Jack the railgun and he loaded and readied it. Dick took them on another Dick route around Queens until Miki proclaimed it safe and he then put together a string of unforgiving New York highways and bridges, the BQE, the Triboro, the Major Deegan, the Cross Bronx—punishing, capricious, crotchety, difficult roads, punctured with potholes and riven with fissures, littered with debris from weaker vehicles, providing no information about how to get anywhere. One wrong turn, even the wrong choice of lane at the wrong moment, and they would be in Montauk or Albany before they could do anything about it, or pinned against a mangled guardrail, waiting for a towtruck driver who would demand cash and lots of it to tow them, inevitably, to some garage on Staten Island.

Dick didn't sweat it—he schlepped packages and furniture all day fantasizing about runs like this one. When he took them under the Apartments on the Cross Bronx at seventy miles an hour and then shot out onto the upper level of the GWB, Miki Mu rested her gun on her lap and punched him in the arm.

"Nice, driving man. How about some tunes?"

Dick hit play on his tape deck, frowned because jazz piano just wasn't right, and ejected Dick Hyman. His fingers found a tape in the ashtray, he popped it in, and Luther Vandross oozed out of the speakers. Miki Mu pulled a tape off the dashboard, ejected Luther, popped in *Diver Down* and gave them some Van Halen. Jack watched the island fall away behind them. He saw the towers of the hospital, and a strand of brake lights on the West Side Highway, and the park on top of the sewage treatment plant, and the steeple of Riverside Church, and the illuminated hives of Midtown and Downtown way off to the south. The four cables that suspended the bridge looked far too thin for the job, as they reached up in arcs attached to the great anchoring towers. Hundreds of feet below, the Hudson was nearing the end of its majestic run, the reflection of the City distorting in its shifts and eddies. And above it all was the sky, the great, open, empty, weightless sky. It was all around them, and instead of being afraid, Jack felt like he'd been released, like he'd found open water, like he could finally move and think and breathe.

Jack got up off the cooler and opened it. There were still a couple Gatorades bobbing in the tepid water. He pulled them out and climbed onto the transmission hump between the front seats. They were halfway across the George Washington Bridge, doing a shaky eighty. The cliffs of Jersey opened up and swallowed them in a short tunnel lined with yellow tile. Jack offered a bottle to Miki Mu who shook her head. He gave it to Dick who touched it to Jack's.

"Fierce Melon in the DickVan!" they toasted. They pulled the sport tops with their teeth and drank all the bold flavor they could handle.

Beyond the Palisades was a delta of roads and ramps that

disbursed the outbound traffic stream from the City into the gulf of New Jersey and the unexplored Rest of the Country beyond. Jack was overwhelmed by the choices: 95, 80, 9W, 4, 17, 46 , Express, Local, Palisades Parkway, Fort Lee. But Dick skillfully navigated the shoals and channels, hidden reefs and wrecks and sandbars without looking at the signs.

"Where is Dick going?" asked Dick.

"White Whale," said Miki, "Hackensack. I've got the Vette stashed there. We'll get something to eat, make sure nobody's following us, then we'll do the swap and you can go."

"Cool. Copy that. Dick loves working for you badasses," Dick gushed.

"Easy. Just get us there. Then you can take off."

"Word, I can drop in on my Ma."

Dick piloted them across an overpass, faked merging onto the Interstate, and put them on local Route 4, speed limit fifty, a doddering, crumbling old road choked with gas stations, motels, car dealers, and off-brand fast food. Somewhere in a token stretch of trees that represented the forest that had once stood there, Dick exited the highway and wove his way through blocks of nearly identical houses, differentiated only by the color of the vinyl siding or the presence or absence of the optional decorative shutters. He negotiated labyrinthine subdivisions of split-levels and blasted down streets lined with faux Tudors set back from the road behind massive hedges of azaleas and rhododendrons. He chugged along a shopping street that boasted Kosher Chinese food and Party Balloons and Louie's Charcoal Pit. At the end, where the stores gave way to more split-levels, the DickVan took a bridge over a muddy estuary, made a left at the Liquor Barn onto a four-lane service road, passed a tire store and a McDonalds, then made a quick left into the safe harbor of the gravel parking lot of the White Whale.

The lot backed onto the brackish water they had crossed on the bridge, and surrounded a small glass block, white-tile-and-stainless-steel building shaped like a cartoon whale. The seats and counter were in the head, the kitchen was in the body, and the tail curled up and over and faced the street. A decades-old neon sign was built into the flukes and buzzed in sequence the words, WHITE WHALE HAMBURGERS, then the outline of a Whale around them, and finally a spout of little burgers from the Whale's blowhole.

"Park in front, Dick. We'll leave the gear in the DickVan, put it in my car later," ordered Miki.

"Copy that," said Dick.

"You're killing me with the jargon, man," said Miki.

"Roger—uh, OK," said Dick.

After making sure the parking lot was free of IROC's, Navigators and GNX's, Dick parked the DickVan in front, and the trio entered the white whale through its gaping jaws.

Herman the grill man greeted Miki Mu, Dick, and Jack with a nod each. Impossibly, there were a dozen stools in the small space, arranged in a horsehoe around the grill, soda fountain, register, and door to the back, and a few more in each corner next to the front door, facing the parking lot. Most were occupied—people sat in groups of threes and fours and their clothes indicated that they worked in a range of professions. Jack saw a cop uniform, a couple of suits, flannel shirts and Mack Truck hats, a Nets jersey and cap. There didn't seem to be any Goldties.

Jack sat down immediately in front of the grill. Miki Mu quietly corrected him, "No Fish. Not with your back to the door," and nudged him along.

Jack quickly moved down the side of the central horseshoe,

taking the stool next to the payphone in the corner. Miki Mu and Dick followed and filled in the seats next to him.

Herman the grill man stood opposite Dick.

"'Sup, Herman."

"Hiya, Dick. Whaddayouhave?"

"Gimme six with cheese 'n onions. Coffee. Fries."

"Six with cheese," Herman repeated. "Fries, coffee!" he called over his shoulder.

A woman's head peered out of the back kitchen, which must have had the same square footage as the soda machine. "Fries, coffee!" she repeated, and disappeared again.

"You?" Herman asked Jack. Jack scanned the menu, a series of pegboards sponsored by Pepsi hanging above the kitchen door. White sans serif capital letters spelled out BURGER and CHEESEBURGER, DOUBLE and DOUBLE WITH CHEESE, FRIES, SHAKES: VAN, CHOC, STRAW.

"Uh, OK. Wow. Six burgers? Sounds like a lot. Um. I guess I'll just have a double cheesburger."

"No he won't," a man in a brown suit behind him corrected. He tapped Jack on the shoulder and said, "I'm sorry to butt in, but you don't want a double. Ruins the meat-to-cheese-to-bun ratio. You want more food, order more burgers, but don't get doubles."

"Thanks," Jack said appreciatively. "I didn't know."

"'Sall right. I didn't mean to be nosy, but I hate to see someone make a mistake like that," said the man, who returned to the conversation he was having with a Chinese guy who was having three different conversations on three different cell phones in three different languages.

"Make that four cheeseburgers," Jack corrected his order.

"Four cheese." Herman repeated. "Onions?"

Jack shrugged.

"Take onions," said Herman, definitively. "Pepsi?"

"Pepsi, sure." Jack went with it. He really wanted a strawberry shake, but if Herman said Pepsi, he would get a Pepsi.

"Pepsi!" yelled Herman.

"Pepsi!" confirmed the woman in the back.

Herman reached below the counter and came up with loose balls of raw meat speckled with pearls of fat. He slung them down on the right edge of the small grill and smacked them flat with his spatula. Then he grabbed threads of raw onion with his fingertips, sprinkled them over the meat, and smacked the patties again. Row by row, he flipped them over and shifted them left on the grill. He set up buns, some with squares of yellow cheese on both halves, some without, and let them warm on the rack over the grill.

Herman kept track of the orders with a complicated mnemonic system he had learned from an ex-South African Special Forces mercenary. He never got it wrong.

When they were done, Herman slid his spatula under two tiny burgers at a time and laid them on the open buns he'd arranged according to the individual orders. The woman from the back emerged with small scalloped paper plates of fries. As she put each plate on the counter, she flashed a quick, self-conscious smile, then hurried away to the back room to make more fries.

Herman tossed a paper plate in front of Jack and announced, "Four cheese. Onions. Enjoy."

Jack examined the mess in front of him. The burgers looked like somebody had already eaten them—they were

steamy, mushy, ugly little things. The buns had partially collapsed from the heat and spilled crumbs of meat, gobs of
melted cheese, threads of onions, and rivulets of grease. A
small pile of pickles in caustic brine steadily ate its way
through the plate. Dick leaned over, opened the lid on one of
the burgers, and squirted on a smiley-face of ketchup for
Jack. As repulsive as it looked, the intoxicating vapors that
wafted from the pile of questionable food were too much to
resist. Jack picked up one of the burgers and discovered that
it was very, very hot.

He held it to his mouth, bit, and chewed. It was moist,
savory and unexpectedly sweet. Jack hadn't realized how
hungry he was. Right then, he was glad that eating burgers
was the job. The first burger was gone in three bites.

As they ate, the seats they had initially occupied filled up.
The woman in the housedress appeared to be a regular, but
the two guys dressed like mechanics in dark blue coveralls
were new to the White Whale. Once they got through the
ordering process, the woman shouted out, "Hey Herman!
Tell my boys here about Colonel Izzy."

"Tell *them*?" asked Herman.

"Colonel Izzy?" asked Jack.

"Shut up and listen," cautioned Miki Mu.

Herman wiped his hairy hands on his apron, scraped his
spatula on the edge of the grill, and approached the counter
in front of the mechanics. "OK. I'll tell 'em."

The hum of conversation in the little metal room tapered
off as everyone pretended not to listen but did anyway.
Herman began.

"So when I first took over this place, they made these

big-ass burgers. 'The White Whale,' right? Freakin' obsessed. They were huge things—it was like holding a dead cow with bread handles, y'know? So that's what I made. Big burgers. But I wasn't satisfied. I wanted to do something special with the stand here. I had to come up with something real unique, 'specially with the competition over there. . ." Herman's gaze fell on the golden arches across the road.

One of the mechanics made a sympathetic *huyng* sound.

Herman nodded, "Yeah. So, first I tried playing around with the bun. I went sourdough, pita, pumpernickel, challah, I tried matzoh, I made a burger hero, I put one on Fig Newtons for chrissake. But I didn't find what I wanted there."

Jack shook his head sympathetically, as if he too had followed the false prophet of the Fig Newton bun. Mostly he wondered if he could go on eating while this guy told the story of his burger Odyssey. Herman picked up on Jack's state of mind.

"Don't stop eatin' jus' 'cause I'm telling a story. G'head."

Relieved, Jack dug back in to his food.

"The next thing I tried was foolin' around with the toppings. I went all the way up that river. I tried the veggies, the guac, the salsa, the pineapple, the cheeses, pizza crap. I got weird. Did Nutella, liverwurst, ice cream, shrimp. I went to Asia, brought back peanut sauce, chutney, and panko flakes. Nothing did it for me. It was all the same old bullshit. Hunk of meat on bread with some whatever on top. But it didn't mean anything. It was driving me nuts. I was ready to try fried chicken."

"Oh no! You never told me that!" The woman in the housedress was horrified.

"Oh yes. I woulda, too, 'cept *he* came in."

"Who?" asked Jack through a mouthful of delicious burger.

"Colonel Izzy, that's who!" Miki Mu called out.

Herman looked at the aluminum ceiling and his eyes clouded over. "Colonel Izzy. He came in here, and I *knew!*"

"He told you how to make these things?" one of the mechanics asked, waving his burger for emphasis.

Herman glared and roared, "No, he didn't fuckin' tell me how to make hamburgers! He told me to sell out and put all my money into his teak plantation in Central America!"

Everyone had a good laugh at that.

Herman was now addressing the entire audience, pacing around the grill and gesturing dramatically. "Colonel Izzy was crazy. He never made any sense. He drove a hazmat tanker. Always hauling benzine and Draino. No, it wasn't anything he said—it was *him!*"

"Ah-ha!" said Dick.

Herman leaned in and looked into Jack's eyes. "You have to understand. Colonel Izzy was extremely handsome. Very intense. Perfectly proportioned. And three feet tall. He had the most amazing hands. Supple. Beautiful. And that's when I got the idea! It wasn't the ingredients—it was the proportions! I got a tiny store here. I decided to make a tiny burger!"

"Genius," exclaimed Dick.

"Yeah it is," agreed Miki Mu.

"I don't know about that, but that's what I did. I always liked this supermarket bun, so I started there. I weighed out the meat on this gram scale I got from my brother-in-law. He used to ride with the Angels. Sold the meth. *Before* he married my sister. Anyway, the cheese food product is Kraft, the onions are from Shop Rite, that's it. Fry 'em up. Just keep them like this, is all."

"Ratios, brah, ratios," Dick said conspiratorially to Jack.

"What happened to Colonel Izzy?" Jack asked.

"Dunno. Gone. Maybe to Central America. Who knows? 'Scuse me. I'll get your drinks."

Jack's first two White Whale cheeseburgers were gone. Only as he wiped his oily hands on the napkin he'd tucked in his collar did he realize that the superheated greasy onions had affixed themselves to the roof of his mouth and were quietly etching his palate. A slurpy draw on his arriving Pepsi loosened them up and sent them down his throat, and he was ready for burger number three.

By now, everyone had been set up and was happily eating. There wasn't any conversation, only a lot of grunts, lip smacks, tongue noise, and slurping. On his third burger, Jack made the mistake of thinking aloud. "I'm gonna need a couple more of these."

Dick heard him, and summoned Herman with a wave. "Two more for my boy over here, Herman!"

Herman nodded and threw two more meatballs on the grill—*smack, smack*.

"There's only one thing I don't get about this Colonel Izzy," mused Dick.

"What's that?" asked Herman as he wiped the counter with a rag.

"How'd a midget drive a semi?"

"I think they've got special pedals. Platforms. Platform pedals."

"Platform pedals?"

"Must be."

Jack stood a ketchup bottle on a stack of fives and thanked Herman. Dick lit two Seaweeds and gave one to Miki Mu on their way out the door.

"OK, Dick. My ride is in the back under the trees. Back the DickVan up to it, and we can do this," Miki Mu ordered.

Jack looked around nervously. "You're not worried about somebody seeing us? Won't it look suspicious, us sneaking around the parking lot with our bags in the middle of the night?"

Dick and Miki Mu exchanged smiles.

"Come on," Miki Mu said as she pulled Jack by the sleeve. "Let's get the car ready."

As they walked around the side of the whale, Jack saw the policeman who had been inside when they first sat down. He was standing by the open trunk of a brown K-car, counting twenties on the spare tire while his dining companion in the bottle-green suit moved boxes labeled EVIDENCE into the trunk of a BMW. Jack and Miki Mu approached a low-slung car parked under the trees. It was covered with a blue tarp bungied under the frame. Next to it was parked a white cube truck. The rear roll-up door was open and one of the guys with the Mack Truck hats was wheeling out a large birdcage on a dolly. The bald eagle inside tried to appear dignified as the cage was lowered and nearly dropped before being stashed in the Dodge Caravan driven by the Reverend George. As Jack and Miki Mu undid the bungies, the Chinese guy popped the trunk of his Maxima and removed a live heart in a cooler. He replaced the cooler with gold bars wrapped in sections of the *Star-Ledger* given to him by The Russian.

Jack peeled back the blue tarp and saw a purple supercharged '77 Sting Ray coupe with "Save our Shore" New Jersey plates that read OG MU.

"Subtle," he observed. "The Maltese will never see us coming."

"It's called *style*, Fish. When they see me rollin' they'll know they're fucked," Miki Mu said.

The DickVan whined up in reverse, and Dick rolled the side door open from the inside. Miki Mu had the trunk of the Sting Ray open, and laid in the long ski bags full of guns, umbrellas, and spears.

"Say 'hi' to your mom for me," said Miki Mu.

"Good luck," Dick nodded and waved, sliding the door closed with a heavy thunk. The DickVan roared off toward Paterson; Miki Mu and Jack took the Parkway south.

Miki Mu was busy. Jack watched her practice opening her umbrella, loading the three-band gun, aiming at an imaginary target, dropping the long gun and picking up the pneumatic as she dove forward. When she could perform the entire sequence in eight seconds, she took the pillowcase off of her head and placed the umbrella on the plastic bedspread. She unshouldered her quiver and removed the spears one by one, examining each point for sharpness and each shaft for straightness before placing it in a row next to the others by the umbrella. Then she put her left arm behind her back and practiced unsheathing the hooked blade that all the Orachalcum Guardians carried from the leather garter on her left ankle. This she could do in less than two seconds. Jack stared in horny fascination. She was a compact, smooth, curvy, very dangerous killer at work on her killing routines, and together they were holed up in a hot-sheet motel on the outskirts of Asbury Park in the long hours before dawn on the day of their terribly important and very dangerous mission. Surely she was in the mood for desperate we-might-not-live-through-this-but-damn-it-we're-going-to-try sex with him?

"I'm not having sex with you," she told him, recognizing the look in his eyes. She put the arsenal on the floor and flopped down on the bed next to Jack. "Ready?" she asked him. He was fiddling with his mini-gun, loading and unloading it, pulling and hooking the single rubber band in clumsy imitation of her weapons ritual.

"Absolutely. Finally going to see some action. Can't wait," he said.

He held his gun in front of him, peering down the spear at a yellowed "Beautiful Boardwalk" poster on the wall. He aimed at bathing beauties, a Ferris wheel, surfers, salt water taffy, and then felt the impact of his hand hitting his forehead as the powerful rubber band released with a *twang!* instantly transferring its potential energy to the spear and hurtling the spinning nickel tip on the steel shaft through the poster, through the paneling and into the bathroom on the other side with a solid *thunk!*

Miki Mu laughed.

Jack got up to retrieve the spear. He found it sticking out of the tile above the toilet, doing its best to pretend that it had always been there, that a spear was as part of the average motel bathroom as the paper sash around the toilet seat and the outlet with the red button for hairdryers. When Jack pulled the spear out of the wall, it made a raspy scraping

sound and released a puff of chalky dust. He turned around
and caught his reflection in the mirror over the sink. Jack
tried a few expressions and poses with the gun to see which
one made him look coolest and most ready for secret-agent
action. When he went back into the bedroom, Miki Mu had
the lights off and a movie on the television—*MacGyver:
Lost Treasure of Atlantis.*

She pointed at the screen. "We gotta get cable in Atlantis.
Look at what we're missing!"

Jack agreed. "There is so much to learn about our own
culture, you know?"

"You should get some sleep," she said. "Gotta be sharp in
the AM." Miki Mu changed the channel and found a *Man
from Atlantis* marathon.

"What about you?"

"Too wired. I'll crash when this is over, or I'm dead,
whichever comes first."

"Yeah, me too," Jack said, stifling a yawn as he lay down
next to Miki Mu. On the TV, Mark Harris was trying to
stop Mr. Schubert from melting the polar ice caps. He was
fighting with Schubert's henchmen at the pillared gates to a
temple, and while Jack watched, the door opened and his
mother came out holding a pan of Deep-C fishsticks, call
ing, "Jack! Come to supper!" Jack pushed past the tussling
men on his doorstep and went inside his house. Johnny
Belmont and Gozo and Jack's brother Joe were sitting at the
kitchen table. They were banging forks shaped like miniature tridents. Mac the bartender served huge glasses of dark
beer and plates of anchovies, then shrunk into Colonel Izzy.
"Teak!" he shouted, "Teak!" until Gozo speared him in the

eye with his now telescoping fork-harpoon. Jack walked out the back door and found himself on top of a huge water-slide. He could see the rings of the real Royal Metropolis around him, bands of white marble slabs and pillars, houses and streets, schools, offices, shops and avenues rebuilt in the ordered, regulated, dull official design mandated and maintained by the Elders. In the dim reaches beyond the outer ring Jack saw the tumbled and broken blocks and beams of his once great civilization now buried under the slime of ages. Massive piles of stone, entire districts and towns, were covered in algae and sponges, encrusted in barnacles, coral, and mud. And car dealerships. And gravel parking lots. And hamburger stands and office superstores and stripmalls selling discount dinettes and oriental carpets and stereo equipment and above-ground swimming pools and supplies, and Jack was driving past all this in a black GTI with a pair of claws on the roof and Chloe by his side. She was laughing and said, "Pull over for a minute!" and Jack did. They got out of the car, which turned into a dolphin, flashed a toothy smile and swam away. Victor Sargasso was standing on a bridge above them. Chloe waved to him, and she and Jack climbed a long flight of stairs to the top, avoiding the man in the puffy down coat and self-made plastic diaper snoring on the first landing while penguins swam all around. The bridge had a view of New York from the twenty-sixth floor that made Jack feel funny inside.

Victor was wearing a Batman suit. He swigged from a bottle of GEOЯGI and passed it to Chloe. She poured the rest of it down her throat and tossed the bottle over the edge and then kissed Victor with a lot of visible tongue. Victor put a box on the white desk in front of him and said, "Open it," to Jack. The lid read POLARIS 360. Inside was an electric eel. Chloe picked it up and shoved the sparking end into Jack's stomach and kissed Victor some more as blue bolts of pain shot through Jack's gut. He doubled over while his internal organs tried to strangle each other and then he stumbled and fell off the bridge, plummeting through the void, falling through the potpourri-scented darkness, screaming in agony, begging for death until he woke up sweating in a New Jersey motel room. He ran for the toilet to purge the six hallucinogenic hamburgers with one tremendous, agonizing push. Tile crumbs fell onto his head like snow.

The next time Jack awoke, thin orange light seeped through the curtains. Miki Mu was absentmindedly drawing a star on his chest with her fingernail. The shape burned as if with light, then faded.

She said, "I'm supposed to go back down for a while once this is finished. I don't think I want to, I've been up for three years. But I'm an OG. The Right Prong. Duty calls."

"Yeah," said Jack. "Yeah."

"The Maltese had you, huh?"

Jack was embarrassed. "I guess. For a while."

"Then they dumped you."

"Yeah."

"Fish—we have to stop them."

"I know. But—"

"But nothing, Fish. They don't know what they're talking about. They only understand the power, not the danger or

the responsibility. The Elders act the way they do for a reason, and it's a good reason, Jack. They don't want to sink
the world again. And we have to listen to the Elders. The
Elders are the Middle Prong, right? That's how the Trident
works."

"Of course, of course. But do we have to stay *so* hidden?
So cut off from . . . all of this?" he made a sweeping gesture
with his arm. "I mean, what if Victor and the Maltese are
really building a new Atlantis?"

"I don't know. Don't care either. Things have been this
way for, what? Twelve thousand years. We hide our power,
even from ourselves. You know that, Lefty. The old world is
gone because we destroyed it."

"Obviously the old world is gone. But we're not part of
the new world either."

"That's the deal, isn't it? The price?"

"But the Maltese—"

"Look, Fish. I don't know why I have to be the one to
remind you of this, but the Maltese made a choice. They
left, OK? When it all went down, most of us died. They
left, and found a way to survive, Poseidon bless them. But
we didn't leave. We stayed. We adapted. We survived and
we made sure that the world wouldn't end again because of
us. And that means hiding and fishsticks and whale-oil
lighting forever and ever. Victor Sargasso made a choice
too. He had a job to do and he didn't do it, and that is why
we are going to kill him. It doesn't matter if he stole one of
the Stars or not."

"OK, OK, Maltese bad, Elders good, Victor Sargasso gets
it, and the Maltese don't. I only wish . . ."

"What?"

"It's dumb."

"No, what?"

"I wish the food were better."

"Fish?"

"Yeah?"

"Don't make me have to kill you, too."

Miki Mu drove into the Shark River Dry Dock and parked the OG Sting Ray behind a sailboat cocooned in blue shrinkwrap. The sky was dark with threatening clouds; there was a metallic scent to the heavy air—even two people from the bottom of the sea could tell that it was going to break and rain hard. Miki Mu and Jack got out of the Vette and looked out at the Atlantisland development site in the Shark River inlet. Jack put the "Atlantisland, NJ—the Mystical Kingdom of Neptune" PowerPoint deck he had swiped from Triton on the hood of the car, and they compared the map inside to what they saw before them. The marketing copy claimed that Atlantisland was a "new city of water and stone," designed according to the exact layout of the lost Royal Metropolis of Atlantis, as documented in Plato's writings. Jack snorted.

"Like Plato knew what he was talking about!"

Miki Mu slapped him in the back of the head and pointed.

The scale of the project was staggering. Through eminent domain, the State of New Jersey had claimed the entire Shark River basin for this mixed-used development: people were evicted from their homes, parks were decommissioned, businesses were bought and closed, streets were demapped, and the very shape of the land was being redefined. Billboards depicting the various rides and attractions that were to be built in Atlantisland rose from backyards, rooftops, parking lots, beaches, and the water—huge, garish depictions of flumes, coasters, waterslides, arcades, malls, restaurants and hotels themed around crystals, sharks, giant squid, classical architecture, Easter Island heads, and alien spacecraft. Heavy equipment, steel girders, big holes, stacks of plywood, and mounds of sandbags were littered around the once picturesque community.

At the far end of the bay, a long cut connected the inlet to the Atlantic. It flowed under Route 35 and the Ocean Avenue drawbridge before passing between two jetties and meeting the sea. The houses that once stood on either side of the canal had been demolished and clusters of new buildings were going up, in roughly pyramid-shaped arrangements. These were called the "Royal Titan Timeshare Community" on the four-color map.

"That's the only bit that looks remotely like our Atlantis," Jack complained.

"Shut up, Fish. This is recon. Serious stuff. Concentrate."

She had a pirate-style spyglass, which she extended and

held to her eye. "This is worse that that monstrosity in the Bahamas," she muttered under her breath.

Jack tapped the map with his finger and said, "Look! They're actually building the Ring Islands!"

And they were. To create the concentric rings of water and land, the banks of the bay were being cut away with backhoes and dredging machines mounted on barges. The material was then sifted and organized in mounds according to granular size—piles of dirt, sand, pebbles, stones, rocks and boulders. In the water, sea walls were constructed out of four-pronged concrete caltrops and huge chunks of rock. The walls outlined the shapes of the islands, which were to be infilled with the rubble from the piles according to the engineer's recipe for firm, stable ground. One of the outer ring islands was still only two bands of concrete and stone that stood a few feet above the waterline. The central island, however, was almost completely filled in, and this was the location of today's ceremony.

The centerpiece of this island would be the Palace of Poseidon, a huge, gold, and many-columned, multi-purpose entertainment, shopping, and dining facility. For now, it was merely an illustration on the billboard that stood in the middle of the island, in front of empty rows of bleachers. Between the billboard and the bleachers sat a temporary stage with flimsy, decorative columns at each corner and a lectern facing the grandstand. Behind the stage stood a huge cast metal statue of Poseidon clutching a trident and a spouting blowfish, which the Triton proposal described as the "signature image" and "benign immortal" who would watch over the "exciting re-creation of Atlantis right here in Atlantisland, New Jersey." The sculpture had been built based on Chloe's model, and it was curiously dull and unfinished-looking.

As Jack and Miki Mu watched, the first ferry reached the inner island and discharged its passengers, who stood around in groups pointing and gaping and making for good seats in the bleachers.

"We'd better get over there," said Miki Mu.

Atlantisland's parking lot was an expanse of gravel deposited and spread by bulldozers across four acres of irreplaceable wetlands. A crowd of people had gathered for the festivities celebrating the largest development project on the Jersey Shore since gambling was legalized in Atlantic City. They were lining up for the ferries that would take them to the central island, and Jack and Miki Mu joined them in the disguises they had cobbled together at a Mobil snack shop: "NJ and You Perfect Together" mesh baseball hats and knockoff Wayfarer sunglasses. They also wore Chlorinator wind breakers from the Pool Supply store and toted jumbo umbrellas fat with weaponry. Families had packed picnic baskets to make a day of it, fathers and mothers and children in matching polo shirts and khaki shorts and boat shoes without socks. Girls with bangs sprayed crisp as baleen leaned on the arms of men with blow-dried mullets. A Girl Scout troop had split up and was moving through the crowd, canvassing for Thin Mint orders. The Sea Girt volunteer fire department was off-duty and ready for a good time. As the line moved, they shuffled coolers of beer along with their feet. A flannel-and-denim cadre of Springsteen fans showed up, as they did for any event on the Shore, just in case the Boss made an unannounced appearance. Everyone hoped it wouldn't rain and had brought along umbrellas in case it did. In the front of the line, Jack spotted several Triton employees, and he carefully avoided anyone that might recognize the AWOL intern.

Despite the ominous weather, there was palpable excitement on the ferry as it slowly made the short crossing. Pleasure boats tooled around the new canals and moats and the islands-in-progress. Seagulls swooped low in the air, and the people on the boat gasped and pointed at each giant picture of a ride as it came into view—THE SPHINXSTER, SINK OR SWIM, ELEPHANTASY ISLAND.

Everyone disembarked at a makeshift floating dock, helped ashore by smiling high school students fulfilling their community service requirement for the National Honor Society. Miki Mu and Jack quickly disassociated themselves from the gawking crowd and made for the rapidly filling bleachers.

Miki took an appraising look and told Jack, "It's perfect—a clean shot. Hurry, there are still some seats left in the top row."

As they walked in front of the stage, the incongruous smell of cow manure wafted over from behind the billboard depicting Poseidon's Temple.

Jack saw Heather sitting with the Entertainment and Exhibition crew from Triton in a place of honor in the front row. He hurried past before she could recognize him. Miki Mu jammed her small butt in next to his on the top bench.

The volunteer fire department sat in the row in front of them next to the Girl Scout troop. The atmosphere was festive and buoyant, in contrast to the low, dark clouds. Jack was caught up in the moment, looking forward to the speeches and the hoopla until he considered his bulging, heavy umbrella and the reasons that he was here.

A special ferry festooned with garlands of flowers and Jersey tomatoes pulled up to the central island, and a parade of dignitaries disembarked. They marched past the bleachers and up to the platform in front of the statue and the billboard. The Mayor of Neptune proudly led the way in her gold-trimmed Jackie O suit. She was followed by one of New Jersey's congressmen, a couple of state senators, and a former Miss New Jersey, still wearing her sash and tiara. Last came members of the local chambers of commerce, representatives of the construction companies, union and mob bosses, and the Shrewsbury High School Marching Band, who were playing a rousing Sousa march perilously offkey.

The dignitaries filed onto the platform and took their seats on folding chairs that were arranged in a semi-circle around the lectern. Unseen, a helicopter chugged, getting louder and louder. It appeared from behind the billboard, low in the sky, and landed in a whirlwind of spray and sand on the edge of the island, opposite the ferry landing. Victor Sargasso and Gozo emerged—Victor tall and elegant, scarf whipping behind him in the wind, Gozo bent and twisted, shuffling with the aid of a cane gripped tightly in his (or her) metal claw. They approached the stage radiating pride in accomplishment and esprit de corps. A sturdy Goldtie followed a few paces behind, carrying a heavy-looking black attaché case. Gozo's hairy white dog jumped out of the copter and lifted his leg to pee on the landing gear, then ran on his little legs to catch up.

Miki Mu leaned over to Jack and pointed significantly at Gozo and Victor as each made a show of not being the first to sit down.

Jack hissed, "You're going to kill Sargasso here, in front of all these people *and* the Mayor of Neptune?"

"No, Fish. *We* are going to kill Sargasso and any Maltese we can in front of all these people and the Mayor of Neptune. Didn't they teach you anything in spy school? We have both cover and surprise working for us. Work fast, hit as many as we can, make sure Sargasso goes down, and jet—got it?"

In a panicked voice Jack asked, "How? How do we get out of here?"

"Fish," Miki Mu gave him a patronizing look. "The whole fucking place is surrounded by water. You *are* wearing your mankini, aren't you?"

After the Shrewsbury High School Marching Band played "Born to Run," the unofficial New Jersey State Anthem, to a standing ovation, the Mayor of Neptune spoke. Her shrill voice overdrove the mike; windnoise and feedback distorted her words, as the tinny PA speakers scattered them across the bay. Jack kept his eye on Victor Sargasso, who was looking smug and self-satisfied, sharing the occasional chuckle with Gozo, who sat beside him, nodding his (or her) head in assent. The Mayor of Neptune said—

> *eeeeeee* Business and the public sectors *pppppppp-op* noble enterprise-ise-ise *iiiiiiiii* cul-

mination of years of planning-ing-ing *grrrrrrrrrnk* our friends at MaltaKnights-ights-ights *nnnnnnnngh* spectacular, *whhhhhoo* not a ground-breaking *schweee* a ground-making *ffffffffiii* rise of a new shhhh first shovel *pop-op-op* thank you-you-you-you!

After the other politicians and the former Miss New Jersey spoke, Gozo took the podium. The Goldtie stood next to him (or her) smiling hard and holding a huge cardboard check. Gozo's voice hissed—

sssss thrillingss occassion *ssss* a new world is born *ssss ssssss* take this gloriouss ssstatue behind me *sssss* Malta for gilding with twenty-four carat *twee* by artisssssansssss of great ssssssskill. I ssss-incerely believe in the *ssssssssssschchpt* tisland*!*

"Didja get that, Fish?" Miki Mu asked intensely, fingering her umbrella.

"It sounded like Gozo swallowed an eel."

"They're taking the statue. Away. Do you understand? They're taking Poseidon. Gozo is giving somebody that big check and leaving with a great big Poseidon—"

Jack finished her thought for her, "—and the Star is in the Statue. Sargasso is taking the big check in exchange for the Star. This whole thing is just for show."

Miki Mu smiled. "You were right, Fish. You were *right*. OK, listen. I'll take that traitor Sargasso. *You* have to stop the Maltese from getting the statue, no matter what happens."

"What's going to happen?"

"I'm not exactly sure, but I called in Bermuda Salvage."

Jack looked around wildly. "Bermuda Salvage? With all of these innocent people!"

In a horrible mental montage of destruction, Jack saw the missing ships and squadrons of airplanes, the collapsed oil platforms and demolished Malibu mansions that were all the work of Bermuda Salvage. Created by the Elders to harvest the booty of disasters under the law of the sea, Bermuda Salvage had become extremely powerful and ultimately unmanageable. Not content with gleaning the bounty of chance, Bermuda Salvage had turned to creating their own disasters to harvest. Making big things disappear under the waves was their specialty.

Miki Mu made a sweeping gesture. "Whatever happened with Sargasso, this abomination has got to go. I don't know what they'll do, exactly, but be ready. Once they do it, there probably won't be much time."

The Mayor of Neptune announced the legendary Atlantis Bull Ceremony.

"Oh gods," Miki Mu groaned and flopped back on the wooden bench. Jack sat forward, eyes wide.

A remix of Holst with a jungle beat pumped out of the PA, the music slapping back on itself a half second later from across the bay. There was a shout from behind the temple billboard and a herd of ten cows came wandering out, clumping their heavy hooves. The crowd applauded appreciatively.

"This is whalecrap! They're supposed to be bulls," Miki Mu slagged. "They couldn't find ten bulls in New Jersey?"

Following the cows came ten men on stilts wearing the flowing deep-blue robes that Chloe had designed. Jack noticed Clive's bald head among them. These were the "Princes of Atlantis," and they were hunting the cows with nooses and Louisville Sluggers. There was an impressed "Oooh" from the bleachers; the volunteer firemen raised their beer cans in earnest salute. For a while, there was a confused shuffle—the princes had trouble landing the nooses on the wandering cows. When one did manage to get a rope around a cow's neck, he never seemed to be able to tighten it before the cow shook it off. The crowd tittered indulgently, and waited for something to happen.

A mythic figure rose majestically above the temple billboard, riding in the bucket of a backhoe. It was Chloe, Jack realized, dressed as the Queen Cleito of her own imagination, with some help from the mad taxidermist the studio next to hers. She wore a mermaid's tail and giant lobster claws with a five-pointed spear attached to one. A crown of interlocked starfish wreathed her colorless hair. She looked down on the statue of Poseidon, the stage full of dignitaries, the cows and the princes and the audience, made a sweeping gesture with her claws, then stabbed down into the bucket of the backhoe with her spear and pulled a bloody calf's head up on its tips. She raised it in triumph above her head and hurled it to the ground where it bounced and rolled, leaving a grisly trail in the sand. The crowd gasped. Clive roped the bloody calf's head around its ears and snapped it into the air. Another prince produced the large golden bowl and a jug of Carlo Rossi Burgundy. Clive whipped the calf's head into the bowl and the other prince poured wine over it. Then to the disgust of the audience, the bowl was passed from prince to prince, each sucking deeply through yard-long Krazy Straws.

From her backhoe perch, Chloe proclaimed: "May the Gods bless this temple, its ten-track waterslide, virtual-reality experience, and glass-walled food court! May Poseidon find our humble offering pleasing, and may he give this mixed-use development his protection! May ticket sales be brisk, and may interest rates stay low! May Atlantis rise once again from the murky depths and regain its place among the civilizations of the air! May Atlantisland, New Jersey, become the premier theme park destination of the mid-Atlantic states!"

This was something the crowd could get behind. They applauded and hooted and laughed as the cows were led away by the NHS kids. Slowly, dramatically, Chloe was lowered behind the billboard. The princes hobbled off on their stilts, and Victor Sargasso stood to mild applause.

Victor presented the Mayor of Neptune with a golden shovel. A worker trucked over a wheelbarrow filled with yellow sand, and the Mayor stuck the shovel into it. Then she dumped a spadeful into a hole in front of the platform that had been left ceremonially unfilled. She raised the gleaming shovel and pumped it in the air in celebration.

As the crowd cheered, the sky opened up in a tropical downpour. Miki Mu unceremoniously opened her umbrella, loaded a .357 powerhead-tipped spear into her three-band gun and fired, hitting Victor Sargasso square in the chest. The impact knocked him over backwards, his scarf flapping and his feet in the air. At the same moment, there was a deep rumble from the far side of the island that shook the bleachers like the minor earthquake it was.

Jack was on his feet, struggling with his umbrella when a bolt buried its head in the seat between him and Miki Mu with a shudder. On the stage, Gozo's Goldtie was cocking a crossbow with his foot and reaching into the attaché case. Gozo made for the helicopter on his (or her) bandy legs. Meanwhile, a rolling wave of water about an inch high had quietly crossed the island, pulling the ocean behind it. Miki Mu dropped the big gun, slung her quiver on her back, loaded her pneumatic and yelled to Jack, "I'm going after that one-handed lamprey. You'd better deal with the statue! Good luck, Fish," and she disappeared under the bleachers.

The audience was becoming aware that something was somehow wrong. Smoldering patches of nervous murmuring broke out in the crowd:

"Was that a *crossbow*?"

"Was that an *earthquake*?"

"Was that part of the show?"

When the next tremor hit, panic and wild screaming erupted all over. People jumped to their feet and started pushing and climbing and standing on heads. They wanted off the island, and they wanted off *now*. The island dropped downward with a sickening lurch.

For the first time all morning the Mayor of Neptune could be heard clearly: "Atlantisland is sinking!"

Jack finally had his gun loaded with a multi-prong galvanized spear. He stood up to get off a shot but was yanked backwards over the top rail of the bleachers. He landed heavily in the gathering water below. As he lay on his back in the muck, he heard the throb of a powerful engine. Tipping his head back, he saw a lobster boat full of men in gold wetsuits reach the rapidly diminishing shore of the island. One was reeling in the grappling hook he had just used to pull Jack down; others were holding crossbows and bracing themselves to land and attack. Jack made for the confusion under the bleachers, crabwalking under the metal supports as he felt the island slip away from under his feet. The water rose faster and faster.

When Jack reached the front of the bleachers, he had to swim under the first couple of rows to get through. He stood—the water was up to his waist. Now, instead of fleeing the bleachers, those that could reach them were trying to climb to the top row where Jack had sat just minutes ago. The dignitaries on the stage clung to the edges as it began to float off its base. Gozo's personal bodyguard had the former Miss New Jersey under his arm and was signaling frantically to the helicopter that struggled to break free of the thickening mud. The smiling NHS kids were trying to direct people to the waiting ferries, which were still moored to the floating dock, which was no longer moored to anything at all and was drifting towards the parking lot. People in private boats and jetskiers tried to position themselves to help. Two Girl Scouts wearing sashes full of merit badges floated by in a cooler that the volunteer firemen had gallantly emptied of ice and beer. A cow swam in circles, lowing mournfully. Then Jack heard the throbbing engine again, and saw the Maltese craft make for the stage where Gozo was shouting and waving his (or her) claw at the statue of Poseidon, which teetered precariously as the pressure of the water shifted it from its base. On the brink of righting itself, it fell with a great splash that nudged the floating stage of dignitaries in the direction of the sea.

Jack knew what he had to do. He removed his jacket and his shoes. *This was the mission.* He took off his shirt. *This was why they had chosen him, trained him, sent him up to the top.* He unzipped his jeans. Eating soup wasn't the job. Drinking with Johnny Belmont wasn't the job. Waking up in Dumpsters wasn't the job. He was the Left Prong of the Trident and stopping the Maltese from stealing the Star of Atlantis was the job. Jack dove into the water, speargun in hand, ready for battle in his blue mankini.

Visibility was terrible in the turbulence below, the water thick with mud and grit. Jack could see that the island was collapsing and spreading itself across the bottom of the inlet. There was another rumble from behind, a grating and a ripping sound, and the island poured away even faster. Bermuda Salvage had unzipped the sea wall, letting the guts of the island fall out. Jack couldn't help being impressed as he kicked hard and swam for the place he thought Poseidon might have come to rest.

Jack felt a hum, a surge, a sustained vibration just beyond his range of hearing that buzzed through his body and got stronger as he swam onward. There was a light ahead, a diffused glow that came from a source on the bottom. Fine bubbles sparkled in the boiling mudquake, and Jack felt a warmth that grew hotter the closer he got to a glint of metal he could just make out in the muck below.

A grappling hook stabbed down in front of him from a

boat-shaped shadow on the surface. Jack quickly swam to the device, pulled it away from Poseidon and hooked it to the frame of a billboard that was anchored to the sea bed. When he saw the boat-shaped shadow move in that direction, he swam back toward the statue. There, below him, was the toppled backhoe, and there, pinned under its twisted arm, he saw a giant claw and a mermaid's tail. *Chloe.* A silvery balloon of air floated up from her mouth. Jack dropped his gun, put his mouth over hers and gave her a deep breath, then set about removing her tail. Behind him, Maltese divers in gold wetsuits plunged into the water, following the grapple line down. Jack was having trouble with Chloe's zipper, and finally he tore into the fabric of her costume with his teeth. The Maltese were fanning out, searching for the statue. Chloe shook her claws, and Jack understood that she couldn't get at the straps. He alternated giving her breaths and tugging at the commercial-grade Velcro binding her wrists.

The Maltese found Poseidon. One of them had lit an oxyacetylene torch and was going at the statue's neck with it. Another was detaching the grappling hook from the angle-iron struts of the billboard. The boat-shaped shadow loomed overhead.

Jack had one of Chloe's claws off, and with her left hand free, she managed to wriggle out of her tail. Jack kicked off the backhoe and pulled her toward the surface. As they ascended, the golden shovel sank past them on its way down.

Their heads broke the surface and Jack could see the lectern bobbing on its back nearby. He pulled Chloe toward it, and she summoned the strength to clamber inside, where she collapsed, coughing and wheezing and spitting up water and phlegm. Jack floated in the spume, holding onto the side of the lectern with his chin resting on the edge.

"I love you," he blurted.

"No you don't," she gasped, "You just fucked me in a filthy pool."

The Mayor of Neptune drifted by in her gold-trimmed Jackie O suit, facedown with a harpoon sticking out of her back. People were screaming from the rows of the bleachers still above water. The volunteer firemen and the NHS students helped them into waiting boats. Sirens wailed from the parking lot. The sea wall of the outer ring island gently subsided into the bay, collapsing backwards in a circle like the Esther Williams swimmers. The massive displacement pushed a tall wave outward in all directions.

"What the hell is happening here?" Chloe cried as she tried to sit up. "Who the fuck is doing this? Terrorists? Environmentalists? Disney?" She took a hard look at Jack. "Who *are* you?" Chloe pointed over his shoulder. "Why do *they* want my statue's head?"

Jack turned to see the Maltese lifting the tarnished head of Poseidon into their boat. He swam toward them, alone, unarmed, useless. The Maltese at the winch saw Jack and picked up a long wooden speargun. He fired wildly over Jack's head and reloaded, but didn't shoot again. The last diver's gold swimfins were still sticking out over the side of the boat when they took off, cutting a white wake in a ninety-degree turn toward the canal and the open sea. A jetski broke from the flotilla of rescue boats and gave chase, a diminutive figure with long black hair at the throttle.

Over the sound of the engines, the screams from the Girl Scouts, the sirens and the rain, Jack heard bitter laughter and the expletive, "Fuck!" from behind him. He turned and swam desperately back to the lectern.

The coffin-like box had taken on a lot of water and was listing hard to port, juddering in the chop. Chloe's giant claw dangled over the side and her head was thrown back. The spear that had been meant for Jack protruded from Chloe's shoulder and pinned her to the wood. She groaned, laughed, and said, "Fuck!" again.

Jack swam to her. She was bleeding heavily, sprawled on her back, wearing half of a Sea Goddess costume, and losing consciousness.

"I wish I had this shit on tape . . . didja see that performance?" she gasped, and her head wobbled to the side. "Look at this . . . it's brilliant! Shot with a spear by a guy in a fucking gold wetsuit . . . battle over a statue . . . Atlantis goes down . . . still got my fucking claw on . . . Ow."

Jack was drowning in guilt. "I'll get you to an ambulance. It looks like you got hit in the muscle. That's good."

"You tried to warn me, didn't you?" she said as she slipped below consciousness. "Cute. . ."

Jack dropped back into the water and pushed the sinking lectern toward the parking lot. As he neared the shore, he saw helicopters, ambulances, National Guardsmen, police. They were questioning witnesses, who pointed and gestured and babbled incoherently about harpoons and earthquakes and being wet. John Johnson was on the scene for Channel 7 Eyewitness News. His pants were soaked to the thighs as he stood with the chaos as his backdrop for the five o'clock lead-in.

The paramedics saw Chloe coming. Jack gave the box a kiss and a push, and as he slipped under the water he heard them barking, "Looks like another puncture! Get her out of that box! Let's get her on the chopper! I need an I.V. over here."

Something bit Jack's ankle. He kicked at it and Gozo's little white dog dog-paddled for shore.

The tide was going out and Jack was pulled with the rush of water, broken equipment, loose lumber, and other flotsam down the long canal. The banks had been lined with wooden bulkheads to keep people's lawns from eroding, and as Jack passed by these were peeling off and pitching forward into the water. The current carried him under the highway and the Ocean Avenue drawbridge, and past the old men fishing in their yellow rain slickers. Jack swam between the red and green lights on the tips of the jetties that reached out into the water like arms trying to hug the horizon. He turned around in time to see the rooftops of the Royal Titan Timeshare Community disappear below the dunes as Bermuda Salvage finished the job. Atlantisland, New Jersey, disappeared from the world with a wet burble. The rain stopped as abruptly as it had started and the sun came out. In the distance, the former Miss New Jersey, Gozo, and the state senators were getting smaller and smaller and smaller.

J ack walked as far as Polski Pork Provisions before he lost the momentum to go on. He stood at the window pondering the myriad ways an animal could be cut to pieces, ground up, and then stuffed back into its own intestines. Jack had been drifting up through Greenpoint along Manhattan Avenue, getting closer and closer to Chloe's studio, not sure why he was going there, not sure where else to go. A lot of things were troubling him. He'd put together a chart in his head:

SITUATION	CATEGORY
Keys no longer opened the doors of the safehouse.	Problem.
Didn't know if Victor Sargasso was alive or dead.	Big problem.
Hadn't prevented Maltese from nabbing Star.	Very big problem.
Gozo and the Maltese might kill him.	Possible problem.
Victor Sargasso might kill him for not killing him first.	Likely problem.
Elders might have Miki Mu kill him for not killing Sargasso and letting the Maltese nab the Star.	Very likely a really big problem.

With all of these issues to occupy him, Jack forgot about the one problem he *wasn't* having at the moment—his breathing, which was really going quite well. The other thing he didn't notice was that while he listed his woes (they seemed as numerous as the varieties of sausage in the window), his hand idly pulled the green Duncan Imperial from his pocket and let it fall, spin, touch the sidewalk, roll forward, and climb back up its string with an easy, rhythmic roll of his wrist. Someone else *did* notice, though, and made a call on the corner payphone, speaking only the word *kreplach* before approaching Jack. He was a boy, maybe fourteen. He wore a black hat, a white shirt, black pants and shoes.

"Hey, Mister Fish," said the boy, throwing a forward pass with his blue Imperial, which snapped back into his palm with a satisfying smack.

Jack was surprised that he wasn't surprised to be personally addressed by this adolescent. "Yes?"

"Get in the car, please," said the boy.

"What—" Before Jack could say *car*, it rounded the corner and pulled up in front of him—an old black Fleetwood limousine with B-ZAR plates. A door creaked open and Jack and the boy climbed in, sliding across the cracked leather bench. Balthazar sat on the opposite seat with his legs crossed beneath him. He was wearing a white robe and red flip-flops and was unwinding the leather straps of a small leather box tied to his forehead.

"Jack-the-Ripper, Tire Jack, Jackie-O, Wolfman Jack, Jack-O-Lantern, Jack Kerouac, Jack Daniels, Jack

Nicholson, The Jackson Five, Jackson Pollock," he said, "Jackie, Jack, would you like an egg cream?"

"Egg. . ." Jack stammered, "cream?"

"Moishe." Balthazar indicated a rack of glasses with the smallest gesture of his hand.

Moishe opened a compact refrigerator concealed behind a wood veneer panel and removed a glass bottle of milk. He took two heavy pint glasses from the rack. He held a glass under a jar of Fox's U-Bet Chocolate Syrup and pumped a squirt into it.

"*Dam!*" Moishe cantillated.

"Hebrew," explained Balthazar. "Blood, it means."

Moishe pumped another squirt of chocolate, "*Tzfardeyah!*"

"Frogs."

"*Knim!*"

"Lice."

"*Arov!*"

"That is, er, like a pack of wild beasts."

"*Dever!*"

"Pestilence."

"*Sh'chin!*"

"Hmm. Boils, that one is."

"*Barad!*"

"Hail."

"*Arbeh!*"

"Locusts."

"*Choshech!*"

"Darkness."

Moishe pumped the last squirt into the glass and said, with finality, "*Makat B'chorot!*"

"The slaying of the first born."

As Moishe poured milk into the glass, Balthazar explained: "The ten plagues visited unto Pharoah, until he would allow Moses to lead the slaves across the Red Sea."

"Oh," said Jack.

"A little teaching device. It helps the pupil maintain the proper count."

Taking a long steel spoon from a drawer, Moishe stirred vigorously with a chopping motion while he blasted the milk with a jet of seltzer. He sprayed and stirred until a light brown mound of foam formed on top of the glass and spilled over the edge. Moishe wiped the glass with a white cloth and handed it to Jack, who politely waited until Moishe had finished preparing Balthazar's egg cream as well. Jack accepted the offer of a straw. Balthazar did not. Jack tried a sip of his egg cream. It was sweet and light; it had a rich, buttery feel to it, with the dry brush of the soda bubbles to finish. Jack looked at Balthazar who had a brown, foamy mustache, which he wiped away with the back of his hand while exhaling a satisfied "Aaah." Jack sighed in agreement.

"Good," Balthazar said, addressing Moishe. "But next time, remember, long, continuous pumps. I can taste your hesitation."

"Yes, Rebbe," Moishe said with downcast eyes.

Balthazar held his glass aloft, turning it a few degrees back and forth appraisingly.

"Another paradox in this strange world, eh, Jack Fish? A dying art. The egg cream. No egg. No cream. And not much real seltzer or U-Bet to be found anymore. Or milk for that matter. It will be difficult for young Moishe to continue the practice, but that only makes it more worthwhile, eh, Moishnik?"

Moishe looked up from the half-pint junior egg cream he was mixing for himself and nodded.

Jack sat back and sipped his egg cream. The rear compartment of the limo surrounded him like a bathysphere— snug and isolated. It was hard to judge speed, motion, time of day, or much else about the world outside. The windows were tinted too deeply to see anything outside the car other than bright lights. A smoked glass partition separated the driver from the passengers. The limo maintained its own parameters of light, temperature, and sound—at the moment, dim, cool, and hushed, with "Flamenco Sketches" floating at the edge of aural perception.

"*Mazel Tov*," Balthazar said, raising his glass. "To your success!"

Jack was stunned, then he broke into cynical laughter, and blurted out faster than he could stop himself, "Success? What are you talking about? I totally fucked up! It was a complete disaster! Sargasso is probably still alive, Miki Mu had to shoot him because I couldn't do it myself after the sushi, the Maltese have Poseidon's head and the Star, and Chloe might be dead—they're gonna kill me—"

Balthazar cut Jack off with an upturned palm.

"Perhaps you suffer from the same delusion as your Elders?"

Jack was too astonished to say anything.

"Give me your yo-yo," said Balthazar.

Jack pulled the green yo-yo from his pocket and handed it to Balthazar.

The rebbe looked at it for a moment, as if confirming something he already knew to be true, then disappeared it into his voluminous robes.

"The yo-yo is very, very old, " he said dreamily, looking at the roof of the car. "How old, nobody knows. Images of yo-yos are found on Greek vases, yo-yos themselves have been found in Egyptian tombs. There are yo-yos in the Wats of Southeast Asia, yo-yos in the deserts of Africa and Arabia, yo-yos in China and yo-yos in the Far North. Such a simple thing, a child's toy, and yet, so many secrets, eh? So much to learn?"

Balthazar produced a blue Imperial still in its packaging and handed it to Moishe who opened it.

"Finger!" Balthazar commanded Jack.

Once again he tied a slipknot and said, "When you can take it around the world, come and see us. We'll be at our usual table."

The car stopped. Moishe opened the door and Jack could smell where he was—the candy and the sweat and the piss and the ocean came pouring in the door, along with the clatter and screams from the roller coaster, and ringing bells from the boardwalk, and honking horns from the Avenue. He was back where he had started.

Balthazar was sharing his teachings. "Jack. Work on your tricks. Smoothness, flow, rhythm, these will give you control. Indecision, imposition, impatience, these will leave you flopping on the string like a fish on a hook and line. The yo-yo wants to spin. You have to let it. It will guide you, and in turn, you will guide it."

Jack got out of the limo. He stood there with the door

open, not sure what to say. Before he could come up with something, the rebbe leaned out and said, "It might be about the yo-yo, it might be about the Star, and it might be about something else, but it's usually not about you. Remember that. Not about you." The door closed and the great car rolled away.

Jack looked around. He was standing next to Nathan's famous frankfurter stand a block off the boardwalk on Coney Island with a blue yo-yo in his hand. He put it in his pocket and started walking when he heard a voice.

"Hey."

Chloe strode up to him with her left arm in a sling and two hot dogs in her other hand. She handed him one. "I wanted to see you so I went looking for that pig, Johnny Belmont. Fucker left town, but that old yo-yo guy at the bar told me I'd find you here today, so here I am."

"Yeah," said Jack, taking the hot dog. "Here I am, too."

He wanted to touch her, but all he managed to say was, "You OK?"

"Yeah," she said. "I'm OK. But why'd that crazy little chick want to kill Victor?"

"Because I didn't." Jack said to his feet. "Is he dead?"

"I don't know. He's just gone."

When Jack looked up, Chloe said, "You think they'll let me on the Cyclone with this thing?" indicating her sling with a tip of her head.

They rode the rollercoaster and screamed with the kids and watched the freaks eat fire and swords, and Jack carefully put his arm around her in front of the shark tank in the aquarium. When Jack couldn't stand it any more he said, "I'm sorry, I have to go. I'll try to come back soon."

"Look, whatever, I don't fucking care," she said, because she did.

They walked up to Brighton where the el tracks kept the street in permanent zebra shadow. There was a car service guy smoking a Newport in his Caprice who said he'd go to Greenpoint for twelve bucks. Chloe and Jack exchanged an awkward kiss that tasted of hot dogs and mustard and then she was gone.

Jack walked around the boardwalk for a while, and finally went down to the beach. There were still a lot of people sitting around on towels and getting wet up to their hips and buying beer from the guys who came around with Hefty bags full of ice and cans of cold Miller. Jack bought a couple beers and lay on the sand propped up on his elbow, sipping the High Life as the sun sank into the sea. Two hairy fat guys spilling out of gold Speedos walked by. Jack tensed, ready to fight or to run. He relaxed when he realized they were only Russians from Manhattan Beach on their way home.

When the darkness was substantial enough, Jack walked down to the water's edge and kicked off his flip-flops, glad to be free of them. He stripped off his I ♥ NY T-shirt and jeans, leaving them in a pile on top of his sandals, knowing it all would be gone, part of someone else's life, within an hour. He turned around and stood in his mankini, his feet in the water, a can of Miller in his left hand, a blue Duncan Imperial in his right. He looked back up the beach at the lights on the boardwalk and the puddle of amber light in the sky above, thrown up by the streetlamps, office buildings, cabs, marquees, neon, traffic lights, cigarettes, newsstands, police cars, peepshows, diners and TVs of the City. He tossed back the beer, put the half-empty can on top of his clothes and, grasping his yo-yo, turned again to face the indefinite continuum of sky and ocean. He took a deep breath of everything he could and let it out slowly through his nostrils and then—

Jack walked into the sea.

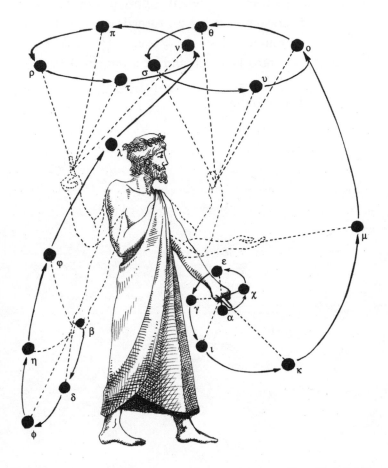

from the *Analytica Yo-Yo Physiognomics Prioria et Posteriora* (Dusseldorf, 1804)

THE SPINNING YO-YO MYSTICS:

Amy, Bryan, Juris, Ailen, Laura, Christy, Whitney, Kathleen, Sabin, Dad, Mom, Rachel, Boss, Nana, Grandma, Neil, Jordy, Jason, Lily, Dan, Miles, Chris, Rault, Sara, Haase, Wednesday, Wonton, Shumai, Lewis, Caroll, Debi, Ignatius, Plato, Schwartzes, Heather, AJ, Monica, Gustav, Orb.

When the finger in the loop is steady, the nature of the yo-yo is to return to where it begins, no matter how tricky the route. It's all in the wrist.

—Balthazar